Praise for the writ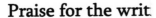

Graceful Submission

"Intense! Exceptional! Wonderful! This is a poignantly penned novel that will take you the reader on a journey into the relationship of a Dom/sub. Once you start reading this novel you won't be able to put it down. I highly recommend *Graceful Submission* as a book you won't want to miss!"

-- Shannon, *The Romance Studio*

"*Graceful Submission* was a joy to read. The chemistry between Grace and Toffer ignites and is smoldering with their combined passion. Melinda Barron captured the characters elegantly and brought them to life."

-- Zoe Knighton, *Romance Junkies*

Graceful Mischief

"*Graceful Mischief* is a nice little quickie that got my motor running. Melinda Barron has done an incredible job writing an exciting and totally hot little treat."

-- Julianne, *Two Lips Reviews*

"Meeting Grace and Toffer was a Halloween experience not to forget. This short glimpse into this couple's life only leaves the reader craving more. Melinda Barron has created a heroine many women can relate too, and a hero we all want."

-- Brandy, *Enchanting Reviews*

Loose Id®

ISBN 1-59632-858-4
ISBN 13: 978-1-59632-858-7
GRACEFUL SUBMISSION
Copyright © January 2009 by Melinda Barron
Cover Art by April Martinez
Cover Design by April Martinez

Publisher acknowledges the authors and copyright holders of the individual works, as follows:
GRACEFUL SUBMISSION
Copyright © February 2007 by Melinda Barron
GRACEFUL MISCHIEF
Copyright © October 2007 by Melinda Barron

This book is an original publication of Loose Id®. Each individual story herein was previously published in e-book format only by Loose Id® and is a work of fiction. Any similarity to actual persons, events or existing locations is entirely coincidental.

Printed in the U.S.A. by
Lightning Source, Inc.
1246 Heil Quaker Blvd
La Vergne TN 37086
www.lightningsource.com

Contents

GRACEFUL SUBMISSION

Chapter One

Note to self: Make sure to avoid eating lunch in teacher's lounge. Avoid Joe Watson at all costs. Don't forget you control your own destiny.

To Do List:

Pick up dry cleaning

Grade at least fifteen more term papers

Stop at Betty's Books to pick up Lindsey's birthday gift

Call Peter to discuss plans for Lindsey's party

"Ms. Kinison?"

Grace Kinison looked up from her desk, cell phone in her hand. "Shouldn't you be at lunch, Jessica?"

"I just wanted to know what I made on my term paper." Jessica LaBlonc's voice was wobbly and Grace sighed. She knew it was hard for the senior to come in and ask about her grade. For Jessica to pass senior English, she had to make at least a B on her research paper. But then again, so did eleven of her fifty-seven students.

But those other students weren't worried about their grades. Jessica was. And the fact that she was concerned pulled at Grace's heart. Jessica had worked hard. She just couldn't grasp the concepts of the class.

"I haven't started on your class yet," Grace replied softly. "I'll know final grades by Friday."

"But that's three days away," Jessica wailed. "I don't think I can wait that long. We turned them in last Friday! Why does it take so long?"

Grace put down the phone and clasped her hands together.

"Jessica, I have fifty-seven papers to grade. It takes time to make sure it's done properly. I'm sorry; you're just going to have to wait." Grace groaned inwardly at the girl's dejected look. "Let me ask you this. How do you think you did?"

The senior bit her lip and then smiled. "I think I did OK. It was hard, though."

Grace stood up and rounded the desk. "If you think you did fine, then don't worry about it. I'm sure that everything is OK. Listen, I'll grade it tonight and let you know first thing in the morning. Fair enough?"

Jessica nodded vigorously and Grace shooed her out the door. She sat back down, picked up the phone and dialed. She pushed send and raised the phone to her ear.

"Watson alert! Watson alert!" Rebecca Shane, the teacher in the room next to her and Grace's best friend, slammed the door to Grace's room and turned off the lights.

Grace disconnected the phone and ran to where Rebecca was standing stealth-like against the blackboard.

"Where is he?" Grace whispered.

"He's coming this way, clipboard in hand. Have you decided how you're going to turn him down without pissing him off? If you make him mad you go from a senior English teacher to a freshman English teacher with one wave of his pen."

Grace's shoulders slumped. "Why won't he go away? I told him two weeks ago that I didn't want the vice-principal's job next year. I just want to keep doing what I'm doing."

Even as the words left her mouth, Grace knew it wasn't true. She didn't want to keep being a senior English teacher. But she didn't want to be a vice-principal, either. She wanted to write full-time, not just from midnight to 3 a.m. All she needed to do was sell one story. One story and she would know that her writing wasn't in vain. Then she could quit her job and live off her savings until she hit the big time. And if she didn't make it big, she would wait tables. Anything was better than working for Joe Watson, who would be principal next year.

She wondered what it would feel like not to have to grade papers every night. Not to have to listen to parents say, "My child says you don't like him and that's why he's failing your class." Not to have to hide from slimy vice-principals.

"Are you listening to me?" Rebecca said. "He may have convinced everyone else that he thinks you're the best person for the job, and I'm not saying that you're not, but we both know that he wants you in the main office so he can stare at those hour after hour."

Rebecca pointed her finger at Grace's chest and Grace blushed furiously.

She wanted to object to her friend's blunt words, but they both knew they were true. Grace was no runway beauty. At thirty-nine, she was at least forty pounds overweight. But she carried most of her extra weight in her chest. And it was the chest that attracted attention she didn't want.

To try and hide her breasts, she wore matronly clothes to work, turtleneck sweaters that were one size too large and long skirts that almost hit the floor. Every morning, she twisted her long auburn curls into a bun and hid her deep brown eyes behind glasses.

That had worked perfectly for years. Until the warm September morning when she and Rebecca had gone to the Pearl Street Mall. Grace loved the Pearl Street Mall. It was one of the best things about living in Boulder. An open air shopping area with stores galore.

The best part was not the shops, though. It was the people. Tourists and residents alike flocked to the area. And it was a perfect place for Grace to sit and people watch, helping her build characters for her books.

For her people-watching escapades, Grace always allowed her "writer" side to come out. That morning she had been wearing jeans and a tank top, her long curls cascading down her back. She and Rebecca had been sitting on a bench, discussing whether or not an older couple they were watching was happy or not (just look at the furrow of his brow, Grace had said, he's disgusted with being here, and with his life) when a low whistle caught their attention.

Standing above them, and staring straight down Grace's top at her double Ds, was Joe Watson. Grace had stood quickly and tried to hide her chest with the notebook she was holding, but the damage had been done.

After that, Watson came by her room two or three times a day. He'd asked Grace out to dinner several times and she'd refused. Then the unthinkable happened. Mark Alt, the principal, announced his retirement and Watson was promoted to his job. Now Watson was after Grace to take the vice-principal's job for the following year.

"Two more minutes until the bell," Rebecca said. "Maybe he stopped at Beaton's room and you're off the hook for another day."

"Fat chance of that. You're nice and thin. Why can't he go after you?"

"My attributes aren't quite as impressive as yours," Rebecca said with a laugh.

The bell rang and Grace let out a deep breath. She turned on the lights and opened the door, and walked straight into Joe Watson's chest.

"Ms. Kinison." His voice was low and Grace stepped backwards. "We missed you in the lounge today. A working lunch? In the dark?"

Rebecca scooted past them with a guilty look on her face. Watson raised his eyebrows at the two women.

"We were just talking," Grace said quickly. "And conserving energy."

Grace cringed as he spoke. "Please come to my office and see me before you leave this afternoon."

Watson left after issuing the command, and Grace turned her attention to greeting her afternoon students. Four more months of Watson. Online publishers were considering several of her short stories. And her book should be ready for submission by the middle of March. Maybe when it was time to sign contracts for next year, she'd know whether or not it had sold. If not, the four more months of Watson turned into another year, and Grace wasn't sure she could handle that.

She sighed as she realized she hadn't been able to call Peter to discuss details about Lindsey's fortieth birthday party. It looked like her evening was going to be full again.

* * *

Grace ran her fingers over the blue bindings of the Nancy Drew book. A first edition *Mystery of the Lighthouse* by Carolyn Keene. A perfect gift for her longtime friend. It was the only book Lindsey was missing in her Nancy Drew collection.

It had taken Betty Rook, the proprietor of Betty's Books, more than six months to locate a copy that was in pristine condition.

Grace smiled as she remembered childhood summers where she and Lindsey had read the Nancy Drew books to each other. They'd laughed over the antics of Nancy, Bess, and George, and acted out scenes in the backyards of each other's houses.

Now Lindsey was living in Brentwood with Peter, her husband. The couple wrote for the highest rated program on TV, *LA349*, a cop show based in Los Angeles. And Grace was a wanna-be writer who was divorced and still living in Boulder.

The book eased the pain of her meeting with Joe Watson. She'd flat out told him she didn't want the job. His unhappiness was very apparent and he let her know that he planned to keep trying to change her mind.

When she'd told him not to bother, a look of such extreme anger has passed over his face that Grace had taken a step toward the door of his office. When the phone on his desk rang, she had bolted out the door and not looked back.

Grace patted the bindings of the book and put it back in its plastic cover. Then she picked up Jessica's paper and got to work.

She had just given the paper a B in her grade book, and watched Jessica's grade rise from an F to a low C, when the instant messenger bell on her computer rang. She maximized the program and frowned as an unfamiliar screen name appeared.

Toffer4U: Hello?

Graceful: I think you have the wrong address.

Toffer4U: I'm Toffer Shelley, a friend of Peter McGinley's. He asked me to get with you about information for Lindsey's party.

Grace slapped herself on the forehead. Peter. She'd forgotten to try and call Peter after the fiasco at lunch. The party was only three weeks away and she'd promised Peter that she'd give him pictures and stories that he could use for anecdotes and decorations. She'd allowed Watson to make her forget the things that were important, like Lindsey and her party.

Toffer4U: Are you there?

Graceful: Yeah, sorry, I was just slapping myself for forgetting to call Peter. Bad day, you know.

Toffer4U: Sorry to hear that. Wanna unload on a stranger? You can pretend I'm whoever you're mad at and yell at me. Just put the caps lock on, and let me know if I need to hold my cheek as if you've slapped me. ;)

Grace laughed out loud. Just like a friend of Peter's to be a character.

Graceful: How do you know I'm mad at someone?

Toffer4U: Isn't that what a bad day usually means, that you're mad at someone at the office?

Graceful: Probably so. But it's not an office. It's a school, a high school.

This time the wait was on Grace's end. She stared at the empty screen and chuckled. That little tidbit had sent Toffer4U back a few paces.

Toffer4U: OK, I think I'm recovered. Please tell me you're not a student.

Graceful: Let's put it this way, the last time I was a student, Reagan was still in office.

Toffer4U: Really? So Miss. Ms. Mrs.? Graceful, what do you teach?

Graceful: It's Ms. Grace Kinison. And I teach senior English.

Toffer4U: Yuck. You're not going to make me diagram a sentence, are you? Or correct my spelling? This could get ugly.

Graceful: I might. What was the noun in your last sentence?

Toffer4U: Is that a trick question? If you look at my high school transcript, you'll see that English wasn't my best subject. I was a "let's bribe the teacher" kinda guy.

Graceful: Those are fighting words in my class. Shame on you.

Toffer4U: Mrs. Williams didn't care. All she wanted to do was sit at her desk and read, and eat the chocolate I brought her. As long as we were quiet and handed in our papers, she didn't mind.

Graceful: Was she close to retirement?

Toffer4U: Way past the time, if memory serves. But I remember her fondly. She never hassled me about anything. And I made a C. Still passing.

Graceful: I don't hassle my students, I teach them.

Toffer4U: Sorry, didn't mean to imply that you did. Forgive me? Shall we move on to the party before I stick my other foot in my mouth?

Graceful: Good idea. And the jury's still out on forgiveness. What exactly does Peter want?

Toffer4U: When the jury comes back, let me know. Just don't send me to the principal's office, OK? I never was very good at bowing down to authority. And Peter wants embarrassing stories from Lindsey's childhood. Pictures that will show how she's changed. Pictures that show what she's done in her life. He'd said you'd have a bunch. You can visit her parent's house and pick up baby pictures. Since the party is a surprise, he thought you and I could work together and she wouldn't figure it out. What do you say? Are you game?

Graceful: Yes, I am. But I have to finish grading term papers this week. Can we talk on Saturday? That will give me time to get out pictures and bring back memories.

Toffer4U: Saturday works for me. How about 1 p.m. your time? That would be 11 a.m. in L.A. We can spend the afternoon together. I'll bring the wine and some hot sauce in case I stick my foot in my mouth again. You bring the food. Something spicy.

Grace felt a warm feeling spread through her stomach. Then she shook her head. A cyber date wasn't a date. It was just talking. And it was planning for Lindsey's party. Still, planning for it with Toffer should be fun.

Graceful: How about Thai?

Toffer4U: Great. One of my favorites. Make sure you get extra spring rolls. And some shrimp rolls.

Graceful: I'll be here. So, Toffer, tell me. Were you a regular in the principal's office?

Toffer4U: Semi-regular. Like I said, I'm not very good at bowing down to authority. I like to be in charge. What about you, Grace? Are you good at bowing down to authority?

Graceful: Authority? The only authority I have to worry about is my boss, who is a creep. But I've pissed him off and I'm afraid the punishment will be severe. Like demoting me.

Toffer4U: Punishment for what? Have you been a bad girl, Grace? Do we need to do some role-playing here? I can be the principal and you can be the errant teacher. Who knows where it will lead? I'll keep the paddle handy Saturday, just in case.

Grace stared at the screen. The feeling in her stomach built and moved to her nipples, which hardened immediately. Toffer's words on the screen made her feel warm, very warm. In all the right places. She shook her head.

Graceful: Never mind. I'll talk to you on Saturday. I've got to get these papers graded.

Toffer4U: OK, for now. But Principal Shelley will be back on Saturday and he'll want an explanation. So be prepared, missy.

His icon disappeared from the screen and Grace laughed. The tingling that had spread to her nipples had made its way south. How long had it been since a man asked her about herself? And why was the idea of talking about punishment with Toffer exciting to her? She didn't even know the man.

She wondered what he did for a living. If she called Peter with her questions, then Lindsey would wonder why she was asking about Toffer. She would just have to ask the man in question on Saturday.

She picked up her red pen and took a paper off the huge stack on her desk. Only thirty-two more projects to grade. At least her Saturday conversation with Toffer gave her something to look forward to while she dodged Joe Watson during the week.

* * *

Christopher "Toffer" Shelley, known as Drake Dawson to his millions of adoring female fans, shut off his laptop and laughed.

He wondered what Grace Kinison was thinking right now. It was obvious that she had a sense of humor. The remark about the jury proved that. Did she think his parting remark was funny? Or did she think he was a jerk?

It had been so long since he'd talked to a woman as Toffer that he'd forgotten how great it felt. Grace wouldn't judge him on his 6 foot 3 inch frame. She wouldn't judge him on his square chin and high cheekbones; his muscles or his broad shoulders; his tanned skin and brilliant smile; or his light blue eyes and dark hair.

She wouldn't know about his ability to charm fans and the press. He could be himself and not Drake Dawson, star of both the small and big screen.

He walked upstairs to his workout room and programmed the stair-stepper. He began his workout with a smile on his face. He wondered if she was submissive, or if she was freaking out right now about the punishment idea. He hoped she was submissive, that she would react favorably to his tendencies. An online submissive was better than none. And Toffer hadn't had a submissive in his life for ages. He'd learned early in his career that letting his dominant tendencies known was risky. He didn't want to see his sex life splashed across the tabloids.

Toffer's cock hardened as he worked out. Getting to know Grace was going to be fun. With any luck, he could make her his online sub. He'd have Thai food delivered to the house on Saturday. And he'd buy a bottle of red wine to sip while he IMed with Grace.

He made a mental note to tell Peter that he'd introduced himself as Toffer, not as Drake. Then he felt a pull at his conscience. Was it fair of him not to tell Grace the truth? He wasn't really lying, per say. He really was Toffer Shelley, legally. Drake Dawson was his professional name.

If she came out and asked him if he was Drake Dawson he would tell her the truth. Until then he was just Toffer. And he was happy that Toffer was going out to play on Saturday with Grace.

Chapter Two

Note to self: Just because you talk with someone online doesn't mean you are attracted to them. No harm can come from a conversation.

To Do List:

Attend faculty meeting

Pick up take-out menu from Thai Palace for ordering tomorrow

Pick up bottle of red wine

Go through and scan photos picked up yesterday from the Murphy house

Try to forget every embarrassing thing I've ever done so I don't incriminate myself tomorrow while IMing with Toffer

Keep up writing streak and finish Chapter Nine of manuscript

The week had been perfect. It had started with her interesting conversation with Toffer. It had continued when she'd given Jessica the good news that, as long as she kept working hard, she would pass senior English. It had hit another high when Joe Watson had gone out of his way to ignore her. The good days had continued when she and Toffer exchanged daily e-mails. She told him about Watson and he told her about life on a TV set. He'd never come out and said it, but she knew that he must be a writer for the show to be such good friends with Peter.

The e-mails had contained subtle hints of sexuality. Nothing too overt, just reminders that he wanted to spend time on Saturday getting to know her better; Principal Shelley was interested in correcting her bad behavior, if necessary.

The week had peaked last night when her IM program dinged with a message from Toffer.

Toffer4U: Hello from LaLa land. Looking forward to Saturday. Don't forget the Thai food. Do you have a scanner so you can shoot me photos? And I want details. Lots of details. And, oh yeah, stories about Lindsey too... <VBG>

Graceful: Scanner hooked up. Teacher has amnesia and can't remember anything about her own life. Sorry. :-(

Toffer4U: Does Principal Shelley need to stand you in the corner? Would that bring back your memory? Please advise.

His comment had made Grace smile. Her fingers were trembling as she'd typed her response.

Graceful: I thought you were gonna bring the paddle? Guess I'm off the hook, huh?

Toffer4U: Hardly. The corner is for after the paddling. And I don't paddle on a covered behind, so be prepared to bare your little ass. If I were you, I would start remembering, really quick.

And his icon had disappeared. Grace had hugged herself, excited about the prospect of a cyber spanking. D/s play had always fascinated her, but she'd never had the chance to try it out. She knew that she would be meeting Toffer in three weeks time when she went to Los Angeles for the party. Would he want to play with her in real life too, or was this just an online flirtation?

She hadn't told Rebecca about the cyber punishment. She had told her about the conversation turning a bit sexy; she just didn't say what direction the sexy part had taken.

"And I've been writing like a fool," Grace told Rebecca Friday at the faculty meeting at lunch. "You wouldn't believe how things have been flowing out of me. I don't know what started it."

Rebecca took a sip of her water. "How about a man telling you he wanted to hear details about your life? That denotes some interest."

Grace laughed. "You think? He was pretty funny. I can't wait to meet him."

Her grin disappeared when Mr. Alt walked to the front of the room. She was going to miss this man. He had been a great principal.

"Welcome to my last faculty meeting as your principal." The emotion was visible in Mr. Alt's voice and the faculty members gasped. "I know that everyone expected me to remain until May, but things have come up in my life that precipitate my leaving early. Mr. Watson is now the principal, effective immediately."

His voice grew low and tears appeared on his cheeks. The crowd grumbled and Alt held up his hands.

"Things will be fine and I'll miss you very much." The crowd rose and clapped and Alt shook Watson's hand and left the room.

"I'm thrilled to be the new head of Gregory Academy," Watson said, a smile on his face. "We've accomplished a lot under the helm of Mr. Alt. Under my leadership, we will go even further. I do plan on shaking things up a bit."

His words sent a chill up Grace's spine. She looked at Rebecca, who mouthed the words, "Hello, little fishes, and welcome to freshman English."

"I'm already working on new teaching assignments for next year." Watson looked around the room. His gaze stopped on Grace and his smile deepened. "We are also taking applications for my new right hand. If you are interested in this position, see me ASAP."

The meeting ended in a smattering of applause and Grace slumped back against her chair.

"You're gonna get screwed, and not in a good way," Rebecca said softly. "You have more experience than half the English department, and he's going to have you teaching the lower end freshman English classes."

Grace felt the breath leave her lungs. Then she sat up straighter and smiled. "I don't care. Nothing can ruin the high I've been on this week. If he tries to screw me, I'll quit."

"And lose retirement money? Are you out of your mind?" Rebecca's blue eyes widened in alarm.

"I won't let him bully me. If he thinks that by changing my assignment, I'll cave into him, he's sorely mistaken."

* * *

Grace stared at the blindingly white snow that draped the grounds and trees. The delivery man had just dropped off her Thai food and she'd poured herself a glass of wine. It was a little early in the day, but she didn't care. She'd looked forward to this all week. Fifteen more minutes until Toffer IMed her.

His comments from yesterday about the paddling and standing in the corner brought a smile to her face. She wasn't sure why. Maybe it just took her mind off Watson and his threats to demote her. Or maybe it was just the idea of submission. She'd thought about it before, but never brought it up to anyone. She'd never even told Lindsey, or Rebecca, about her secret fantasies. She'd tried to propose the idea of bondage to Jesse, her ex, who had promptly shot her down.

Grace took a sip of wine and then filled her plate with food. She'd just taken a bite of a spring roll, when her IM button pinged.

Toffer4U: Good afternoon, Gracie.

Graceful: Hi, Toffer. How are you today?

Grace laughed. A week's worth of e-mails and it was like they'd known each other for years.

Toffer4U: Fine. Just polishing up my paddle. <g> How's your lunch?

Graceful: Good. Yours? And I've been good. You don't need the paddle. <squirm>

Toffer4U: We'll see. I want to get the party business out of the way first. Then you and I can play a little, get to know each other better. And talk about the punishment. Do you have photos for me?

Grace took a deep breath as she read the message again. Ten minutes ago the idea of a cyber paddling had been fascinating. Now it scared her half to death. Of course he wasn't here. But in three weeks, she would be in Los Angeles, and the threatened spanking could turn into the real thing. She set down her wine glass and sighed. This could be fun or this could be very scary.

Did she really want to go here? Or did she want to put a stop to it, immediately. If she put her foot down, they could plan the party and be done with it. But if she said yes, they could explore something that she'd always been fascinated about. And since she didn't know him, she didn't have to be shy, or worry about what he thought about her weight. Not yet, anyway. She needed to remember that this was a friend of Lindsey and Peter. So surely he wasn't a creep. Hopefully.

Peter trusted him enough to ask him to help with the party. That counted for something. But Peter wasn't going to discuss sexual things with someone he'd never met. The IM ping shocked her out of her thoughts.

Toffer4U: Grace? Are you still there?

Graceful: Yes, I'm here.

Toffer4U: Did I scare you?

Graceful: A little.

Graceful: OK, a lot.

Toffer4U: Hum…but are you tempted?

Grace bit her lip and stared at the screen. Then she tentatively typed in *yes*. Her hand moved toward the enter button, and then pulled back, before she finally reached out a finger and hit send.

Toffer4U: Good. Hold on to that feeling. Now, about the photos…

For two hours, they laughed as Grace told stories of her and Lindsey's childhood that included camping, whitewater rafting, horseback riding and reading. She shot him a copy of the first story they'd written together, a horrible rip-off of the Nancy Drew stories that he promised to read later that evening.

Around three p.m., she reached the end of her scanned photos. She took a deep breath as she stared at the last one.

Graceful: This is Lindsey and I just after my wedding. She was my maid of honor. Of course, the marriage turned to garbage, but it's the best photo I have of the two of us in recent years.

She'd debated about whether or not to send that photo. After all, it showed her in all her glory. When she'd sent everything else, she decided it was a good idea. Toffer would get the chance to see her, to see that she wasn't beautiful and model-thin. She held her breath as the file uploaded to his computer. If he forgot about the punishment discussion after seeing the photo, then she'd know that he wasn't impressed with her body. Better to get it out in the open now.

Toffer4U: Is that your husband standing next to you?

Graceful: My ex-husband, yes.

Toffer4U: I can see why you left him. He doesn't deserve someone as lovely as you are.

Graceful: <blush>

She sighed and chewed on her lip. No derogatory comments about being fat, no "nice tits, baby."

Toffer4U: So are we done with the work, any more photos or stories about Lindsey that I need to give to Peter? We've done our duty for the afternoon?

Graceful: Yes, I think so. :-)

Toffer4U: Good. Before we go any further, I want to make a few things clear. I'm a Dom. Do you know what I mean by that?

Grace stared at the screen, her heart beating wildly. She'd known that already, but she was impressed that he came right out and said it. The idea made her squirm in delight.

Graceful: Yes, I've read about D/s before.

Toffer4U: Have you thought about submitting to a man?

Grace took a deep breath and sighed. She couldn't believe this opportunity was being given to her. It was thrilling. And it was frightening.

Toffer4U: Grace?

Graceful: I've thought about it before.

There, she'd said it. It was out there. There was no taking it back.

Toffer4U: Good. Do you want to submit to me? Do you want to do exactly as I tell you, without question? Do you want to be my cyber submissive? When you come to L.A., we can play for real.

Two minutes went by as Grace fought the butterflies in her stomach, and the thoughts that ran through her brain. She'd wanted this, fantasized about it. This was her chance. She couldn't pass it up. She typed in *yes* and hit enter. A smiley face popped onto her screen, and then a message popped up that made her eyes bulge.

Toffer4U: Take off your clothes, Gracie.

Graceful: WHAT?

Toffer4U: Now. Take them off right now. You're not allowed to question me. Do exactly as I say. Let me know when you're totally naked.

Grace stared at the screen, her heart racing a mile a minute. She hadn't been naked in front of a man in ages. Of course, she wouldn't be naked in front of Toffer. But it felt like it. She bit her lip again. At this rate, she'd chew them off before the end of the day.

She'd said she wanted to be his cyber sub. What did she expect? Of course he'd want her naked.

Graceful: Toffer, I...

She hit the enter button before she finished typing.

Toffer4U: The longer you wait the harder I'm going to punish you when we meet. Do it now.

* * *

Toffer sat back in his chair and smiled. He could just imagine Grace in her house, nervous about taking off her clothes, even though there was no one with her. The idea made him hard as a rock and he gently stroked his cock as he waited. He'd thought about proposing webcams but had decided against it. It was more fun this way. There was more anticipation. More mystery.

It was a good three minutes before the IM button pinged and he knew that she'd been debating whether or not to follow his order. He also knew that since she was hesitating, it meant that if she said she was naked that she wasn't lying.

Graceful: Toffer?

Toffer4U: Are you naked?

Graceful: Yes.

Toffer4U: Good. You must call me Master now. Do you understand?

Graceful: Yes. Toffer, this makes me very nervous.

Toffer4U: Good. And that's strike one. I'm going to keep a running count. When you get to L.A., you'll get licks from the paddle according to how many strikes you have. Be a good girl. How do you address me?

Graceful: Master.

Toffer4U: Excellent. Tell me your fantasies.

Graceful: Just like that?

Toffer4U: Yes. And be honest with me. I expect nothing less than total honesty because that is what I will give to you. Now tell me what you want done to you. Tell me what you expect from a Master.

Graceful: To be dominated. I have no experience, so I don't know what happens.

Toffer4U: But you've fantasized about it. You said so yourself. I want to hear your fantasies.

Graceful: Yes, Master.

Toffer's cock hardened even more and he groaned. He hadn't been called Master in so very long.

Graceful: I want to be tied up.

He smiled; bondage was something that he loved.

Toffer4U: We can do that. What else? Don't make me drag it out of you.

Graceful: I want you to spank me.

Toffer4U: LOL. Not fair. We've already talked about that. Tell me two other things you've fantasized about. And be HONEST.

Graceful: Blindfolds.

Toffer4U: I like that idea, too. That encompasses the whole trust issue. One more and then we'll move on. Don't be embarrassed to tell me. Remember, I'm your Master now.

Graceful: I've always fantasized about being fuc...

Toffer frowned as the incomplete message appeared on his screen. Then a big grin spread across his face.

Toffer4U: Fantasized about what, Grace?

Graceful: Forget that, I meant to hit delete, not send.

Toffer4U: Tell me. Were you going to say fucked from behind? And I don't mean doggy style.

Toffer waited for the replay. He knew that's what she wanted, and he was sure she was blushing at his crude words. She wanted him to take her in the ass. He loved that she was embarrassed to admit it, because it meant that no man had ever taken her that way. He stroked his stone hard cock. If he didn't stop, any minute now he would shoot off in his jeans.

Toffer4U: Grace? Answer me.

Graceful: Yes, Master. I want to be taken anally. I've always dreamed about it.

Toffer4U: That's good, baby. Relax for me. It's gonna be all right. You'll be begging for it before I do it, trust me. Now, take your laptop to your bedroom and lie down on your stomach in the middle of the bed. Stop by the bathroom and pick up a hairbrush on your way. Let me know when you're in position.

He quickly shed his jeans as he imagined her walking toward her bedroom, naked, her large breasts unfettered by a bra. He'd been impressed by her photo. He couldn't wait to suck them before he fucked the deep cavern that ran between the orbs. He knew they would be soft and hug his cock wonderfully as he pumped into them.

He stroked his cock and smiled as the ping sounded.

Graceful: I'm there.

Toffer4U: You have the brush?

Graceful: Yes, Master.

Toffer4U: Put a pillow under your hips so that your ass is high in the air. I want to know that you're ready for the spanking you're going to get today. The one that you're going to give yourself since I'm not there to do it.

* * *

Grace stared at the screen. Had she just read that right? She looked it over again and blinked. Yes she had. He wanted her to spank herself. How was she going to do that? She stared at the brush she'd picked up. It was large with a smooth wooden back. It would sting; there was no doubt of that. But how did he expect her to spank herself? When she'd picked it up, she thought he'd have her look at it while he talked about spanking. She never expected she'd be spanking herself.

Toffer4U: Grace, I'm waiting. And I'm not a patient man.

Graceful: Toffer, I can't spank myself.

Toffer4U: Strike two. I am no longer Toffer. I am your Master now. I won't tell you again. And yes, you can. Reach around with the brush and slap it against your ass. Do it a few times and then let me know how it feels.

Grace worried her lip and then slapped her ass with the brush. It stung slightly, but she was surprised that it felt so good. The sting shot straight to her clit and she wanted to come, now. Was she really doing this? Spanking herself at the request of someone she didn't know? She brought the brush down harder and moaned softly. Wetness was pooling onto the pillow below her. This was so erotic. She couldn't believe she was actually doing what he said. She slapped each side a few times. Her breath came in rapid gasps.

She imagined Toffer sitting at his house in Los Angeles. Was he hard? Did this excite him as much as it excited her? She slapped her ass a few more times and groaned.

Graceful: Master?

Toffer4U: Yes?

Graceful: I did it.

Toffer4U: Good girl. How many times? Did it sting?

Graceful: Just a few. And yes, it stung.

Toffer4U: Good. Did you do each side?

Graceful: Yes.

Toffer4U: Do ten on each cheek. Hard. Imagine that it's me holding the brush. Your Master, spanking you. Punishing you for not remembering that I'm your Master and not Toffer any more. You're submitting to me, Grace. Doing what I want. Do it now.

Grace didn't hesitate this time. She brought the brush down harder with each swing. She imagined Toffer standing behind her, imagined that it was him slapping her ass with the brush. And it excited her. Excited her more than anything had in years. After she'd delivered the final stroke, she reported her success to her Master.

Toffer4U: Good girl. Tell me how it feels. Tell me what you were thinking about.

Graceful: It stings. And I was thinking it was you. I wanted you to spank me.

Toffer4U: And I will, Gracie. Be patient. You have a three-part assignment for tonight. First, I want you to stand in the corner naked for ten minutes. Stick your nose against the wall with your hands clasped behind your back. When your time's up you can bring yourself to orgasm. Do you want to come? Are you wet for me?

Graceful: Yes, Master.

Toffer4U: Good. Very good. Think of me when you play with your clit. Secondly, I want you to shave your pussy for me. Entirely bald. Understand?

Graceful: Yes, Master.

Toffer4U: And third, I want you to write a few paragraphs on why you want to submit to me, why the idea of being a submissive appeals to you and what you hope to gain from it. And I want you to be specific. We'll IM tomorrow at eight.

Grace stared at the screen. What did she hope to gain from this? She wasn't sure why the idea of submission appealed to her; she just knew that it did. She'd have to do some serious soul searching tonight.

Toffer4U: Tomorrow at eight sharp. And make sure you're naked.

His icon disappeared and Grace stood and walked toward the corner, her stomach in knots as she looked at the clock and began to form the list in her mind.

Chapter Three

Note to self: Submission doesn't mean weakness; it means exploring your wants and desires and being strong enough to give control of yourself to someone else.

To Do List:
Write paragraphs about submission for Master
Do more research on D/s on the Web
Be naked by eight
Try to evict the butterflies that have taken up residence in my stomach

Grace turned her rear toward the bathroom mirror and bit her lower lip. There were no real marks from her spanking from last night. But she knew they were there, the lingering ache from the spanking she'd given herself under

Toffer's direction. No, not Toffer, she corrected herself, Master. She's spanked herself under Master's direction.

She sighed as she turned toward the mirror. Her naked mons looked strange to her, but she was proud of herself for following Master's direction to the letter. She'd stood in the corner for ten minutes, feeling wonderfully naughty as she put her nose against the wall. Then brought herself to orgasm, screaming Toffer's name as she went over the edge.

After that, she'd started on her reasons why D/s appealed to her. She'd stayed up most of the night trolling websites to find out information on submission to see if she could explain her attraction to the idea. She'd been surprised to find herself agreeing with so much of the information that she'd read. But the thought of discussing it with Master was scaring her half to death. Her hands were shaking as the clock moved toward eight.

At least he was letting her do it through instant messaging. She wasn't sure she would be able to voice her reasons out loud. Writing them had been hard enough.

The IM program dinged at eight sharp. Grace took a deep breath and looked at the screen.

Toffer4U: Hello, Gracie. Are you naked?

Graceful: Yes, Master.

Toffer4U: Good girl. How are you feeling today?

Graceful: Nervous.

Toffer4U: And how did your writing go?

Graceful: It was a little difficult. I gave it a lot of thought.

Toffer4U: That was the idea. This little exercise serves several purposes. It will give me a better understanding of what you want in a D/s relationship. It will help us get to know each other better as we discuss the ins and outs of our relationship. It will also help us build trust; that's the most important thing in a D/s relationship. You have to trust your Master. Do you trust me?

Graceful: It seems weird to say yes, since we haven't met face to face. But, yes, I trust you, Master.

Toffer4U: I'm glad to hear that. Now, upload your paragraphs to me and we'll see what's what. While I'm reading, I want you to play with your nipples and clit. But don't come. Every orgasm you have from now on will be under my direction, and only when I give you permission.

* * *

Toffer stared at the words that filled his computer screen. Grace had done her duty well. She'd written three concise paragraphs that showed that she'd spent a great deal of time thinking about the subject, which was exactly what Toffer wanted her to do.

He imagined her lying on her bed right now, stroking her clit and pulling on her nipples. Soft moans would be coming out of her mouth. He took a drink of water and re-read the paragraphs.

The idea of sexual submission fascinates me on many levels. I've thought about it for several years, and even suggested the idea of bondage to my ex-husband, who promptly called me a freak. So I buried any feelings that I had, until you came along.

Emotionally, I want to give over control to you because, if truth be told, I want to experience kinky without the guilt that comes with it. Knowing that I'm doing something because you want me to will do that. I don't know if that's the right reason, but it's the one that I've come up with after a few hours of soul-searching. I imagine that this type of relationship brings a mental connection like I've never felt before. And, I want to feel it. By opening myself up sexually, I feel that I can open myself up mentally, too, and make a bond with another person.

Physically, and I know this is where you want me to get specific, I want to experience stimulation that goes beyond the normal realm of sex. I like sex, and I enjoy contact with another person. I want to experience some extremes, including spanking, bondage, and anal sex.

Toffer smiled to himself and looked at the clock. He'd give Grace a few more minutes to stew, to wonder what he was thinking about what she'd written. He wished she was here in the room with him right now. He'd have her sign a contract and then he'd spank her little ass until she was screaming in pleasure. And he knew that she would be.

He and Grace were a match. The only problem was the 2,000 miles that separated them. His cock was straining against his pants. In his mind's eye, Grace was kneeling on the bed in front of him, her hand between her thighs, begging him to let her come. He stroked his hardness and smiled, and then put his fingers on the keyboard again.

* * *

Toffer4U: Grace? Have you allowed yourself to come? Remember you have to have my permission.

Grace turned toward her laptop, wiped her fingers on a towel and sighed. She was so very, very wet, and it had been hard not to come at the idea of Master reading her letter, but she hadn't.

Graceful: No, Master. May I have an orgasm, please?

Toffer4U: No. You wrote a good letter, little one. But on the physical side, you only named off the things we'd already discussed last night. I was serious when I said I was keeping a record for when you're in California. That's three marks.

Grace stared at the screen. Was he serious? Then she shook her head. Of course he was serious. That's what this was all about.

Graceful: I'm sorry, Master.

Toffer4U: Right off the top of your head, tell me five things that you want to experience as a submissive. You have one minute.

Her hands shook as she racked her brain. What could she tell him? This was where trust came into play. She had to open up, and she had to do it now.

Toffer4U: You have forty seconds.

Graceful: Hot wax. Orgasm delay. Punishment.

Toffer4U: That's two. We've already discussed punishment. You have 27 seconds left.

Graceful: Nipple clamps. Role playing.

Grace shook her head. One more. She only needed one more. She didn't want to disappoint him on what was technically their first outing together. What else did she want?

Toffer4U: Fourteen seconds. If you go over your time limit you'll be applying the hairbrush to your backside again.

Graceful: Blindfolds. Wearing a collar and a leash.

Had she really just said that? Grace felt her breath coming in ragged gasps. She'd just given this man permission to attach a collar around her neck and lead her around on a leash. She should be horrified. Instead, she was absolutely thrilled that it had come out.

Toffer4U: Good, Gracie. A collar denotes ownership, and you will belong to me. How are you feeling right now?

Graceful: Nervous. Very nervous.

Toffer4U: Are you wet?

Graceful: Yes.

Toffer4U: Come for me. Ride it out. Stroke that clit and pull on your nipples, and make noise. Think of me there, watching you come for me, watching the passion rip through your pussy.

Grace moved one hand between her breasts. She twisted her nipples and dipped her free hand into her wetness and pulled on her clit, moaning out her pleasure as she worked her nipples and clit. She was so hot that, she came instantly, bucking her hips off the bed as she imagined Master standing behind her, applying a flogger to her backside, urging her to come harder.

Toffer4U: Was it good?

Graceful: Yes, Master. So very good.

Toffer4U: What were you thinking about when you came?

Graceful: You.

Toffer4U: And what was I doing?

Graceful: Whipping me with a flogger.

Toffer4U: I'm stroking my cock right now, Grace. Tell me what you'd do if you were kneeling in front of me.

Graceful: I'd suck you.

Toffer4U: Explain it to me. In detail.

Grace was still reeling from her orgasm. She closed her eyes and imagined herself on her knees, Toffer's hard cock in front of her mouth.

Graceful: I'd open my mouth and swirl my tongue around the head, lapping at the slit, tasting you.

Grace waited for Toffer to answer and then mentally slapped herself when she realized his hands were busy. She decided it was time to go into full-blown writer mode.

Graceful: You're so very hard. I can feel you as I slide my lips over the head and take your cock into my mouth. You're hard and throbbing as you slam into the back of my mouth. You taste so wonderful as I suck you down. Master, come in my mouth, please. Fill my mouth; I'll swallow it all, I promise.

* * *

Toffer worked his hands up and down his cock, his breath ragged as he read Grace's words. She was a great writer; that was for sure. He could almost see her in front of him, taking him deeper and deeper into her mouth; her head bobbing up and down on his dick.

He almost came when her promise to swallow appeared on the screen. But he didn't want it to end so soon. He slowed his pace as she described how good his cock felt in her mouth, how he filled her and that she'd never tasted something so wonderful.

Toffer4U: Grace, you're doing a fantastic job. Don't forget my balls. Run your tongue around my balls.

Graceful: I will, they taste so very good. They're full, and feel like they're about ready to burst.

You ain't kidding, Toffer thought as he quickened his pace and read her descriptions of running her tongue around his sac.

Graceful: Master? Will you feed me your come?

Toffer came, and he came hard, his seed spurting over his hands and stomach. At this rate, he'd sprain his wrist before Grace made it to L.A.

Graceful: Master?

Toffer4U: Yeah, I'm here. Close your eyes, Grace. Lie back and wait for the IM ping. Keep your hands to your sides. I want you to be imagining your first spanking from me.

I want you to wait for me to recover from that stupefying orgasm. Toffer took a deep breath, went to the bathroom to clean himself up and then returned to his desk. He wanted Grace to wait a little bit longer, her mind wandering through the possibilities that awaited them.

He needed to think of a name for her. He always renamed his subs; gave them a name only he would know. They always told him that it made them feel loved. Made them feel like they belonged. He'd come up with something fitting for his new playmate.

Toffer4U: I do believe you're a born submissive. That was very well done.

Graceful: Thank you, Master.

Toffer4U: I'm going to set some ground rules. Break these rules and punishment will follow. And I don't have to be present to punish you. You belong to me 24/7, but you will follow my rules explicitly from 5 p.m. to 6 a.m. Monday through Friday, and all weekend. If you have to work late, send me an IM or an e-mail. I won't interfere in your workday. Do you own a thin robe?

Graceful: Yes.

Toffer4U: When you come home from work, I want you to strip naked and stand with your nose in the corner for twenty minutes every day. That will allow your mind to cross over into your submissive role. Stand with your nose pressed in the corner, your legs spread and your hands clasped behind your back. After that, you will bring yourself to orgasm with your nose pressed against the wall. Then you may wear only a thin robe, unless you have plans for the evening. You must receive permission from me before making any plans, though. Do you understand the rules so far?

Graceful: Yes, Master.

Toffer4U: Good girl. I'm going to send you a box of toys. It should be there by Tuesday. Don't open it until I call that night.

Toffer took a deep breath. It was risky calling Grace on the phone because she might recognize his voice. But he wanted to hear her voice; he wanted to listen while she came, listen while she slapped a hairbrush across her ass at his request.

Graceful: I understand, Master.

Toffer4U: I have to go to a roast tomorrow night, and probably won't be home until very late, which would make it very, very late your time. That means you're on your own tomorrow. Remember to stand in the corner. Then send me an e-mail describing how it felt. You may bring yourself to orgasm by hand only, no toys, before you go to bed. Make sure you sleep naked. Any questions?

Graceful: No, Master.

Toffer4U: Goodnight, Grace. Keep your fingers off your pussy unless you're following my instructions, understand?

Graceful: Yes, Master. Goodnight.

And the screen went blank.

Chapter Four

Note to self: It's all right to be excited about getting yourself off when you're doing so because your Master told you to. What He says is law.

To Do List:
Pay electric bill
Turn in grades
Proof-read last three chapters of novel
Watch roast program and try to figure out which man sitting at the LA349 table is Toffer

Grace checked her watch. It was another twenty minutes until the TV program came on. She put the finishing touches on her edits and closed her computer. As per Master's instructions, she was wearing her short silk robe. And she was cold. She turned up the heat and then turned on the TV. She laughed when she remembered Becca's words from that morning.

"You got laid."

Grace had laughed and tried to deny it, but Becca said she was "grinning like the proverbial cat who swallowed the canary."

Despite Becca's insistence to know if Grace had "had sex or just bought a fresh supply of batteries for your vibrator," Grace had not told her anything.

Instead, she'd floated through the day, smiling at all her students and blithely ignoring Watson's attempt to ruffle her feathers by putting a list of the teachers requesting senior English next year, with her name blatantly absent from the list, in her box. Then she'd come home, stood in the corner for twenty minutes and brought herself to orgasm with her nose against the wall.

Following Master's directions had brought her great pleasure. The minute she'd stripped and pushed her nose in the corner, wetness had pooled in her pussy, and her clit had throbbed. It had been absolute anguish to keep her fingers from drifting south before the twenty minutes was over.

The roast he was attending tonight was for Robert Gray, a well-known actor who was the co-star on *LA349*. It was his sixtieth birthday and the roast would be attended by major Hollywood stars.

Grace scanned the TV screen. She smiled as Lindsey and Peter came into view, sitting at a table with several men and women that she didn't recognize. Two of the men looked as if they were attending the event unattached, unless they were attached to the men sitting next to them, which was entirely possible.

Also sitting at the table was Drake Dawson. Grace smiled as he leaned in to talk to the beautiful blond model sitting next to him, who was obviously his date. Drake was so gorgeous that he made Grace's mouth water. The blond batted her eyes and smiled seductively and Grace found herself wishing it was her.

Get over it, Kinison. He's not Toffer. And that's who you want. You want Toffer, your Master, the man who stood you in the corner today. She shifted her gaze back to the two men sitting next to Peter. They were both in their mid-thirties or early-forties, which would make them about the age of her new Master. Both men were attractive enough, dark-headed with bright smiles.

She closed her eyes and tried to picture each one of them with a flogger in his hands. Neither man fit her picture of her Master. The camera panned to the second table where everyone seemed older than what she had thought her Master would be. A third table of *LA349* actors and workers provided one more man for her consideration; this one a blond.

A search of her imagination showed that she could see this man with a flogger in his hands, see him attaching a collar around her neck. She shivered and pulled her robe closer. A smile flittered across her face and then, suddenly, an image of Drake Dawson took center stage in her brain.

He was wearing tight blue jeans and a dark T-shirt. One hand was on his hip and the other one was pointing toward the floor, where he expected her to kneel. She could easily see the handsome man as Master, and a powerful one at that.

She closed her eyes and felt his hand caress her cheek as she knelt, the words "good girl" floating through the air.

Grace shook her head. Right. Toffer wasn't Drake Dawson. A man like Drake Dawson didn't hide behind an alias. Every woman in the U.S. wanted to get into his pants, and from the looks of the beautiful woman sitting next to him, he was loving every minute of it.

Grace sighed. It had been a mistake to try and put a face to her Master. For her, at this moment, it was more important what he did for her mentally than physically. She turned the TV off and went back to her computer to write.

* * *

His cock was hard, again. And it had nothing to do with the beautiful blond sitting next to him. It had to do with Grace. All he could think about was her naked, standing in the corner. Toffer shifted in his chair and flashed one of his famous smiles at Giselle, the said blond, a stunning model who was instantly recognized by the utterance of her first name only. She was in a tiff because she'd offered to give him a blowjob on the way to the roast and he'd declined. He didn't want another woman sucking on his dick. He wanted Grace.

The roast couldn't end quickly enough. He wanted to get home and check his e-mail, see how Grace's first day of standing in the corner for him had gone; See how hard her little clitty had become while she played with it at his request.

Toffer had spent more than $1,000 on toys. He'd had a box shipped to Grace, and a box shipped to his house for when she was in California. He couldn't wait to see her pussy filled by the glass cock he'd found. The cuffs and harness would fit perfectly. And the flogger would leave beautiful marks on her behind.

He shifted in his seat again and gave a token clap when the first speaker took the stage. Under the table Giselle's hand landed on his knee and began inching toward his cock. He put his hand down and grabbed hers, leaning over as if to kiss her ear.

"Don't."

"Why?" Giselle pouted. "It wouldn't be the first time I've jacked you off at one of these boring events. This will make the time fly faster."

She tried to free her hand and Toffer held it fast.

"I said, don't."

"If you're going to be a stick in the mud, then I'm leaving," Giselle hissed into his ear. "I want some dick. The only reason I came to this boring thing was the thought of playing with your cock before, during, and after. I expect a good fuck tonight."

"Sorry, you'll have to go and find someone else to fuck you."

Ever the show person, Giselle sat back and smiled at him. Then she whispered an apology to the table, picked up her purse and left.

Peter raised his eyebrows at Toffer, who shrugged his shoulders. It was better this way. If he hadn't made plans to attend this event with her weeks before, he would have come alone. He wondered if Grace had sent her e-mail describing her orgasm.

Toffer pulled out his cell phone and connected to the Internet. A grin broke out when he saw her name in his inbox. His cock hardened even more as she described how she'd stroked her clit, pinching it gently as she imagined him watching.

"I'm so wet, Master. It's almost like a river has moved between my thighs. You've done that, the thought of you, the idea of submitting to you. I only came once, like you said, and can hardly wait to come again before I go to bed. I can't wait for tomorrow when my package arrives and we can talk face-to-face, so to speak."

She ended the e-mail with her phone number and a promise to lick him like a lollipop, and swallow every last drop of his sweet offering. Toffer looked at the list of speakers. His speech would end the evening. He figured he had an hour before he had to take the podium. He memorized the phone number and went to search for a private room.

* * *

Grace stretched and reached for the phone. After her second orgasm for the evening, she'd burrowed down into the covers and fallen asleep quickly. A glance at the clock showed that it was after eleven. The ID revealed a number she didn't recognize and she debated about whether to answer.

On the third ring she clicked the on button and whispered a greeting.

"Grace?"

"Yes?"

"I believe the proper address is yes, Master."

Grace's heart beat double time.

"Master?"

"Are you naked, as ordered?"

"Yes, Sir."

Oh lord, oh lord, oh lord. This wasn't supposed to happen until tomorrow night. I wasn't ready for this.

"I thought you were busy this evening."

"I am. But I thought I'd take a break. I want to talk to my little lollipop girl. That's what you said; you'd lick me like a lollipop. Are you wet?"

Grace dipped her fingers between her thighs, although she already knew the answer to the question.

"Yes, Sir."

She parted her folds and moaned as her fingers found her hardened clit.

"Did I say you could do that yet?"

Grace pulled back her hand. "How did you know... No, Sir. I'm sorry."

"That's OK. It's just more reason for punishment when you get here. You touch yourself when I say so, not before. Do you have any candles? Long, tapered ones?"

"Yes."

"Go and get one, and hurry."

Grace ran down the hallway, pulling a long red taper from its holder on the counter and raced back to bed. She couldn't believe he'd called tonight. It was like a dream come true. His voice was deep and dreamy.

"I'm back, Master."

"Good. I don't have a lot of time. Lie on the bed with your legs spread. Then rub the fat end of the candle along your slit. Don't make contact with your clit."

Moans filled the room as Grace followed his instructions.

"Does your clit want attention?"

"Yes, Master."

"Do you remember when I said that punishment doesn't always involve spanking? Sometimes punishment involves denial. Keep your hands off your clit."

Grace sighed. Her clit throbbed with need. She grabbed the bed sheet with her fist to keep her hand from drifting to her core.

"Fuck yourself with the candle, Grace. Stick the fat end into your luscious pussy and fuck yourself with it, hard."

"Master, I can't..."

She wasn't ready for this. She needed another night to prepare. Another night to basically "perform" for her Master.

"Now. I don't have a lot of time and I want to hear you moaning when I come."

Grace took a calming breath. *Just think of it like a vibrator. Your Master wants this, and you don't want to disappoint Him.* She moaned loudly when she pushed the candle inside her wetness. It was cold and hard and despite her original misgivings, it felt wonderful. She moved it back and forth slowly.

"Master. Oh, Master."

"Tell me. Tell me what it feels like."

"Hard, smooth, oh lord, so very good. Please, Master, let me touch my clit. Let me come."

"No, not yet. Push it in as far as you can, and then hold it there. Just lie back on the bed when it's buried deep inside you."

It was all Grace could do to follow his instructions. She wanted to come, needed to come.

"I'm about to come, Grace. I'm stroking my hard cock, thinking of you licking it like a lollipop. When I've come, I'm going to go back to my friends in the main room. Then I'll think about you, lying in your bed with a candle buried deep in your pussy, buried in you because I want it to be."

His breathing was more ragged. "You're on the honor system for this. If you can lie in bed for fifteen minutes, perfectly still, then you can come. If you move an inch, I want you to take the candle out, clean up, and go to sleep. I'll want a report tomorrow night and I'll expect you to be totally honest. Do you understand?"

His words were husky, and seconds after Grace said yes, she heard him moan out his orgasm. How she wanted to be there so she could watch, see him in his passion; passion induced because she'd done what he'd asked her to do. The sound of his pleasure almost pushed her over the edge.

She took a deep breath and held it to keep herself from climaxing. She focused her thoughts on lying still, and the thin chain of self-control almost snapped when Master's deep voice sounded in her ear.

"Fifteen minutes, Grace, starting after you turn off the phone. I'll talk to you tomorrow night." Then the line went dead.

Grace turned off the phone and sank into the mattress. She could feel the candle inside her, her folds throbbing around the hard wax. She wanted to move it in and out of her pussy until she came, and she knew she would come hard.

Think about Master. You want to be totally honest tomorrow when you tell him that you did as he said. She started to count seconds in her head, smiling to herself as she imagined Master standing near the bed, watching her fight the urge to complete what he'd started.

She focused her mind on counting seconds the way her mother had taught her. The number followed by the word Mississippi. One, Mississippi; Two, Mississippi. The candle seemed to swell. The throbbing in her clit turned into a full-fledged pulse. Her nipples felt like hard diamonds. She fought the urge to move by focusing her thoughts on Toffer, on what he was doing. He was surrounded by his hotshot Hollywood friends, and he was thinking about her lying in bed with a candle in her pussy.

After a few minutes that image faded and Master stood near the bed, a flogger in his hand. "How many minutes have gone by, Grace?"

"Nine."

He was gently moving the flogger against his jean-clad legs. "Keep counting. Be a good girl. Count, Grace. There's another minute gone by. What a very good girl you are. Only six more minutes and you can come. You can come hard."

His imagined praises strengthened Grace's resolve and she closed her eyes. Did that count toward movement? She hoped not. Another sixty Mississippi's passed, and then another, and the pulse in her clit turned into a pounding. She wasn't going to make it. She had to come. Now. Only four more minutes and she felt like she was going to cave.

"I'm so disappointed in you, Grace."

No. No. I won't do it. Nine, Mississippi. Ten, Mississippi.

"That's it, Grace. Keep counting. Think about how much sweeter your orgasm will be because you waited, because you followed my instructions."

Grace focused inward. She wouldn't disappoint him with her failure. She centered her feelings on pleasing Master and continued to count. When fourteen minutes had passed, she smiled and fought the urge to shorten Mississippi to miss.

When the final sixty-Mississippi came, Grace arched her hips off the bed, thrust the candle in deeper and came, her fingers pinching her clit as she screamed Toffer's name. Would he punish her for that? For screaming Toffer instead of Master?

When she finally settled her hips back on the bed, she gently stroked her aching clit and another orgasm rolled through her, this one sharper than the last one as she fucked herself furiously with the candle. When she was done she took several large gulps of air and pulled the tapered wax from her body.

She'd never come so hard, and never twice in a row. Her clit still throbbed as if it was suggesting a third orgasm, and Grace shook her head. It was late, after midnight. She needed to clean up and go to sleep. She wondered what Toffer was doing at that moment. Had he forgotten about her lying in bed, following her instructions, or was he checking his watch, fighting the urge to call and see if she'd been successful in following his orders?

Grace padded to the bathroom and laid the candle on the counter. She could see her juices glistening on the wax. The wetness was proof of her ability to follow Master's instructions. The thought brought a huge smile to her face.

Chapter Five

Note to self: Don't imagine trouble where there is none. Allow yourself to be happy for a change.

To Do List:
Stop by grocery store for eggs and bread
Review grades
Continue work on novel
Be home by five to sign for package from Master
Don't open it until he calls!

Grace took a sip of her soft drink and stared at the box on her table. It was hard not to tear into it and see what gifts Master has bestowed on her. But she'd made it through the fifteen minutes last night and she would make it through today.

Even as excitement about the package raced through her mind, she couldn't help but think about work. Watson had summoned a number of her students to his office in regular intervals during the day. In total, fourteen pupils had been called out. And Grace couldn't help but notice that all of them were either failing, or on the verge of failure, in her class.

Seven of them had gone from failing to passing with their term papers; four of them were on the edge; and three were so far gone there was no way they could catch up. She wondered what Watson was up to. None of the students had said anything to her when they'd come back in the room, although all of them had appeared nervous.

Finally, when Jessica had come back from the office, Grace had asked her if anything was wrong. Jessica had looked worried, darting her eyes down and shaking her head vigorously. But Grace knew she was lying. Watson was up to something, Grace just didn't know what it was.

She pushed thoughts of Watson to the back of her mind and stared at the box. Her fingers were itching to open it, see what was inside. She was sure that Master had bought some wicked toys for them to play with, and she wanted to find out exactly what he had in mind.

Before she could give in to temptation, Grace pushed the box away and sat down at the computer. She had two hours before Master called, and she wanted to do more than a little bit of writing before it was time to play.

* * *

When the phone rang around seven, Grace picked it up without looking at the ID. Becca's voice caught her by surprise.

"I debated about whether to call you, but decided that as your friend I didn't have a choice."

"That's an interesting way to begin a conversation."

"Watson is after your ass."

Grace laughed. "I think we've already established that."

When Becca didn't laugh, Grace felt her chest tighten.

"What do you know?"

Becca's deep breath made Grace even more uneasy.

"A parent of a mutual student called tonight. He wanted to know how long you've been taking bribes for grades."

The living room spun around as Grace sank into a chair.

"What? You have got to be kidding me. No one will believe him." The phone remained silent and Grace shook her head. "Becca?"

"Sweetie, you know I don't believe it, but this parent thinks it's true. Word around the school is that Watson called in students all day to see who knew what. The parent I talked to had a student who failed your class last year, and therefore, didn't graduate."

Grace gulped. Dominic Barlow was the only student who'd been forced to graduate at mid-term this year for failing to pass her class last year. And his father was a big-shot businessman around town.

"Becca, tell me exactly what Mr. Barlow said."

* * *

Toffer looked over the array of toys on his bed, checked his watch and smiled. Three more minutes until he talked to

Grace. He wanted to call her exactly at eight, let the anticipation build for both of them.

Last night had been fantastic. She had only balked a little at the idea of fucking herself with the candle. And he knew without asking her that she'd waited out the fifteen minutes totally still on her bed before bringing herself to orgasm. And he was sure it had been a whopper. Little Miss Gracie was a born submissive.

He could tell from the inflection in her voice, just her saying the simple word hello, that something was wrong.

"Tell me."

"I did what you asked, Master. I..."

"Not about that, not now. Tell me what's wrong."

Grace felt a catch in her throat. "I underestimated my new principal. He wants to get me into bed. I refused. Now, I may be out of a job."

"You were fired? That's sexual harassment, you know."

"I could never prove it. Watson is questioning my students, asking those who have failed, or are close to failing, if I offered to give them good grades for money. A student of mine who failed last year told his father that he failed because he wouldn't give me money. The Board of Trustees will start a full-fledged investigation, I'm sure.

"I haven't done anything wrong. I would never, ever, ask a student for money or accept a bribe. I became a teacher to help people learn; to try and instill a love of reading and writing in young people. To say I would take a bribe negates all my work. It just makes me sick to my stomach."

Toffer could tell she was fighting back tears. Her pain and anguish made him see red. He wanted to hop the first plane to Colorado and pop Joe Watson in the mouth.

"This is definitely harassment. You could go to the board members, tell them how he ogled you and only wants to get into your pants."

"I don't think they'd believe me. Even if Becca backed me up, they would think that she would say anything to help me."

"Baby, I thought you were ready to quit anyway."

"I am, but not like this. An accusation like this would keep me from ever going back to teaching, if I ever needed or wanted to."

Toffer took a deep breath. His anger building by the minute.

"Quit. Just go in tomorrow and quit."

"I can't do that, I have a contract. Plus, I don't want my students to suffer because of this. I'm just going to go in tomorrow and calmly discuss it with him."

Her crying was audible and Toffer felt his anger bubble over. How had this happened so quickly? He'd known her for a week and he wanted to hold her in his arms and never let her go.

"Take a deep breath, Lolly."

"Lolly?"

Toffer laughed. "Lolly. That's my name for you. In your last e-mail you told me you wanted to lick me like a lollipop. So you're my little Lolly-girl. Lolly for short."

He smiled when Grace's laughter came in short gasps, showing him she was trying to get her crying under control.

"Let's role-play what you're going to say tomorrow. We can go over the conversation and prepare you for confronting Watson. Planning will keep you calm when you talk to him."

"Tell you what, I'll be Watson." Grace could hear the laughter in Toffer's voice.

Grace's laughter grew stronger and Toffer joined in.

"You don't want to be me?"

"No, baby, I don't want to be you. I want to be inside you. But that can wait. I'm in my office, waiting for you. Knock and come inside. What's the first thing you're going to say?"

"Joe Watson, you're an amoral bastard with a lying tongue."

"Hum, something tells me that doesn't set the right tone. Shall we try again?"

Chapter Six

Note to self: You are strong and independent. Don't allow Joe Watson's lies to bring you down. And don't under any circumstances allow this situation to come into your classroom.

To Do List:
Talk to Watson after school about the false accusations
Have dinner with Becca to discuss situation
E-Mail Toffer after meeting with Watson

Grace stiffened when the office aide came into her class before lunch to replace her so Grace could "attend a meeting in Mr. Watson's office."

Her role-playing with Toffer last night had been very helpful. They'd stayed on the phone until two a.m. going over various scenarios of the meeting, depending on what

Watson would say and how he would react to her statements.

When the conversation had drawn to a close, Grace had sighed.

"So much for a wonderful evening playing with the toys you sent me."

"We'll save it for tomorrow, I mean, tonight. Make sure you don't open the box. E-mail me after the meeting, and then call me after your dinner with Becca."

Now, Grace stopped outside Watson's closed office door. She took a deep breath and knocked. When the door opened her bravado disappeared. Watson was sitting behind his desk, a smug smile on his face. Sitting opposite him was Frank Medina, president of the board for the academy, and Bart Barlow.

Medina stood and held out his hand.

"Grace, thank you for joining us. We have a bit of a situation here that we need to discuss."

"So it would seem. I would have liked to be included in this conversation from the beginning, not joining in after everyone has obviously already given an opinion. That puts me on the defensive and makes me guilty until proven innocent."

A blush spread across Medina's face. "I apologize for that. But I assure you, Grace, there will be a full investigation. I would like to hear your side of the story. Please, take a seat."

Grace nodded to Watson and Barlow. Neither man had stood when she'd walked into the room. Watson looked calm and self-righteous. Barlow's hands were clutched in his lap, his lips thinned in anger.

"I want her fired, right this minute. And I want my son's transcripts changed to take the F she gave him off. That bitch kept my son from going to CU this fall and made him miss a season of football."

Grace stiffened, and then closed her mouth when Medina held up his hand.

"Mr. Barlow, I respectfully request that you watch your language. This is a meeting to discuss accusations, not for a final ruling on charges filed, because no charges have been filed. I agreed to let you stay while I talked with Ms. Kinison because you assured me you could hold your tongue. If that is not the case, then you need to leave. Now."

"Someone has to represent my son's interests," Barlow hissed.

"And I will tell you again, that this is not a hearing," Medina replied. "What I would like is for you to calmly tell Ms. Kinison what you told Mr. Watson and myself. Then, I will give her a chance to respond. From there, I will decide whether to take this issue to the board or not."

"Fine. A few days ago, Dominic told me that Ms. Kinison told him last year that unless he paid her $1,000 that he would fail her class. Dominic told her that he didn't have that kind of money and couldn't get it. She told him the amount was non-negotiable and when no money was offered she failed him. End of story."

Grace shook her head. "Why did he wait almost ten months to make this accusation?"

"He's a kid. He was scared. But the more he thought about it, the angrier he got. He missed an entire football season because of you. He lost a scholarship."

"Dominic lost a scholarship, Mr. Barlow, because he expected me to pass him because of his, and your, status in town. I refused. That's the real story. You and I had this discussion last May."

"That's before I knew you tried to blackmail my son."

"Grace, tell me about Dominic's grades," Medina said.

"Dominic is a smart boy," Grace said. "But he refused to apply himself. He failed to finish his term paper, and refused to read the novels we were reading. He said his future was in football and that he didn't need to read Shakespeare."

"What can you tell me about any conversations you had with Dominic about his grades?"

Grace looked at Watson, who was silently watching the proceedings. She could tell that he was enjoying every minute of it. She was so very happy for her practice with Toffer last night. Despite the fact that Watson wasn't participating, their rehearsal helped tremendously with her nerves.

"I talked with Dominic several times about his grades. He said I wouldn't dare fail him because his father wouldn't allow it. He said he was above doing homework."

Medina raised his eyebrows. "I have trouble believing, Mr. Barlow, that Dominic would wait so long to say anything. Did he give you a specific reason for bringing this up now?"

"One of his friends, Mark Stanson, is in Ms. Kinison's class right now and is failing because he won't pay her."

Grace felt her stomach drop to her knees. "That's not true. Mark, like Dominic, refused to do his work."

"Mr. Stanson provided me with this term paper, which he said you refused to take." Watson laid several sheets of bound paper on his desk.

The blood drained from Grace's face. "That's a lie. He turned in an outline and notes, but never a final paper."

"Then what is this, Ms. Kinison? This term paper has Mr. Stanson's name on it." Watson's smug look deepened. "Could it be that the paper came without the requested $1,000?"

Toffer's voice resounded in her brain. *"Don't let him get to you, Lolly. You're better than that. Be a good girl and you'll get a reward tomorrow night. Lose your temper and you'll get punished."*

"I don't know, Mr. Watson. But I can assure you that Mark never turned a paper into me. He told me that he thought the assignment was useless and he didn't have time to finish it."

"I find that very hard to believe, seeing as how Mark knows what happened to Dominic," Watson said.

"Fire her," Barlow said.

Medina shook his head.

"It doesn't work that way, Mr. Barlow. I will speak with members of the board, confer with our attorney, and we will see what action needs to be taken. But I can assure you that before any action is taken, there will be a full investigation, if we find it warranted."

Barlow stood. His voice was calm and steely as he locked eyes with Grace.

"You'd better find it warranted, Mr. Medina, or I'll sue your school for all it's worth."

Medina stood and offered his hand, which Barlow shook. He glared again at Grace and left the room at a brisk pace.

"Mr. Medina, I promise you that I would never ask for money for grades." Grace was impressed that her voice sounded so calm.

"I'll be in touch, Grace." He nodded at Watson. When he was gone Grace turned to Watson.

"I hope you're happy, and that Barlow is paying you a lot of money to ruin me."

"Why, Grace, whatever do you mean? Remember, it was you who said just last week that I wasn't worth your attention? Why would I be worth Barlow's attention?"

Grace opened her mouth and then closed it when Toffer's voice resounded in her mind. *"Grace, behave."*

"You realize that the school will suffer because I refused to sleep with you? That the students will suffer? Are you so selfish that you don't care?"

"This meeting is over. Go back to your classroom, *Ms. Kinison*, while it's still yours."

* * *

The corner seemed like a haven that evening. Grace stood naked, her nose pressed to the cold wall as her day replayed in her mind. Barlow's angry face and Watson's haughty smile were the worst of the memories. Medina had been supportive at first, and then suspicious when Mark's term paper had been laid on Watson's desk.

Becca had been sweet and sympathetic at dinner. And Grace had not cried all day. Now as she stood naked for her required twenty minutes, the tears began to fall. Fifteen years of work down the drain because she wasn't attracted to Joe Watson.

Part of her wished she could go back to that fall day and replay the events. If Watson hadn't had a glimpse of her chest, maybe he wouldn't have developed the obsession that he had. They'd worked together for years and he'd never noticed her. It was just her Double Ds that had put her in his sights.

She cried softly and when the bell dinged to mark that her time was up she stayed where she was, crying softly. She was supposed to orgasm now, but the desire was not there. She sniffled and shook her head. It was Master's orders that she orgasm. If she didn't she would disappoint him, and although he wouldn't know for sure she would.

Her fingers drifted south, and as she parted her folds, she realized that for the first time since she'd started her standing in the corner for Master she wasn't wet. She rubbed gently, trying to excite herself, replaying the sound of Master's voice in her ear.

The phone rang just as the first tendrils of wetness seeped from her folds. Toffer's name on the display made her smile.

"Hello, Master."

"I didn't know if you'd be home yet."

"I just finished my twenty minutes, and was starting to bring myself to orgasm."

"Stop. We'll play later. First, tell me about what happened today."

Grace told him about their meeting, and about how students stared at her all day and whispered behind their hands.

"Even if the investigation proves that I'm innocent, there will still be people who think I'm guilty...that I took bribes for grades."

"Don't put the cart before the horse, Lolly. Perhaps Medina will prove to be a smart guy and see this for what it is: Revenge for bruising Watson's male ego."

Grace agreed, even though she wondered if that would really happen.

"You were a good girl," Toffer said, causing her to smile for the first time that day. "Go and get your box of toys. Sit in the middle of the bed and undo the seals, but don't open the box."

Grace bounded off the bed and located the box and a pair of scissors. She cut the tape and fought not to peer inside.

"Can I open it now?"

Toffer's laugh filled the line. "Put your phone on speaker, take out a toy one at a time and describe it to me."

The first toy pulled from the box was a vibrator. "It's about seven-inches long, and it's red."

"What's next?"

Grace reached inside. "Nipple clamps attached to a long chain with a third clamp at the other end."

"A clit clamp." Grace shivered as Master's words rang out. She looked at the golden clamp and imagined it on her clit. It would provide a pinch of pain that she was sure would turn into intense pleasure. She'd never thought about using a clamp on her clit.

"We're going to save the clit clamp for when we're face to face. But the nipple ones will be used quite a bit before you get here. There's a few more. Tell me what else is there."

She shook her head, and quickly pulled out another vibrator, this one long and slender; leather wrist and ankle cuffs; a large, round paddle; and, finally, a set of three butt plugs, each one larger than the last.

"There are quite a few toys here, Master."

"What we don't use now, you can bring with you when you come to L.A. I had some things sent here, too, so you have that to look forward to. We'll start off with the clamps. Lie flat on the bed and attach one clamp to each nipple. Twist them around until they are hard little pebbles, then attach it fully. Do it now, my Lolly-girl."

Grace massaged her breasts. Her nipples were already hard, but they hardened even more as she twisted them, imagining Master's fingers pulling on her nipples.

She moaned loudly when she attached the first clamp. "Ouch, ouch."

"Good girl. Don't pull it off; leave it there. Does it feel good, Lolly?"

"Yes, Master. It hurts, but, yet…oh." Grace bit her lip against the sharp pain.

"Good. Do the other one."

Trying to keep her mind off the intensifying pain in her left nipple, Grace quickly attached the right one. The combination of the two sent her senses reeling and she moaned out Toffer's name.

"That's gonna cost you. How do you refer to me, Grace?"

"I'm sorry, Master."

"We'll take care of that when you get here. Tell me how it feels."

"Hurts. Sharp, shooting pain that feels, it feels…"

"Don't be afraid to tell me it feels good, Lolly. If you don't like it, then we need to look for something else."

Don't like it? Grace thought she might shoot through the room from the bliss the clamps caused. "It feels wonderful, Master."

And it did. Under Master's direction Grace pulled on the chain, whimpering as the pain turned into intense pleasure.

"Go clean your new vibrator. Use the red one, Grace. Then find some batteries. Hurry back."

"Can I take off the clamps?" The intense pain was becoming uncomfortable.

"Do as you're told. Now."

Grace took the red vibrator, cleaned it with soap and water and loaded it with batteries.

"Let me hear it, Lolly."

She turned the vibrator on and tried to concentrate on the sound. Anything to take away from the powerful pounding in her nipples.

"Rub it on your clit and talk to me, Lolly-girl. Tell me what you're feeling."

"It hurts, my nipples, I need to take them off. Please, Master…oh lord, oh. I can't. I need…"

"You need to do as you're told. Talk to me."

"It's so powerful. It hurts, but, yet, it feels…"

"Good? Just wait, baby. You're gonna love where this takes you. Fuck yourself with the vibrator. Imagine that it's me, that I'm above you, pounding myself inside your pussy. You're so tight. So warm. Yielding. Fuck yourself with one hand and pull on the chain with the other."

Grace bucked her hips into the vibrator, her free hand pulling on the chain until she cried out in need, but in need of what, she didn't know. On the one hand she wanted to stop the pain by taking the clamps off. On the other hand the fasteners on her nipples were causing the most intense pleasure.

"Master, I want to come."

"Not yet, Lolly-girl. Just keep rubbing and pulling."

Grace's breathing was ragged, her hold on her orgasm barely there. She wanted to come…needed to come.

"Master, *please.*"

"Please what, Lolly? Be specific. Tell me what you want."

"Please let me come. I want to come. *Please.*"

"Put the vibrator right on your clit and pull the chain, *hard.*"

Grace did as he said, then shuddered as words "come, Lolly," registered in her ears. White hot lightning bolts of pain/pleasure spread through her as the clips pulled her nipples, she tossed and turned, finally bringing herself up on her hands and knees as the most potent orgasm she'd ever felt had her screaming, "Master, Master," over and over as she rode the waves of pleasure.

"Come back to me, Lolly. Take a deep breath."

Unintelligible mumbles came out of Grace's mouth and she could hear Toffer's light laughter.

"I take it you enjoyed your first real taste of submission?"

"Yes, Sir," Grace gulped out as she tried to gain control over her senses. She'd never felt anything so intense, so fantastic in her entire life. Was it the physical feelings that pushed her so far over the edge, or the bond that she now felt with Toffer? She had a feeling it was a mixture of both.

"I've never. Felt. Anything." She took several deep breaths and collapsed on the bed, a large smile spreading across her face.

"Shush, little one. It's all right. Breathe deep."

Grace didn't know how long she struggled to regain control over her breathing. Her clit was pounding and her nipples felt as if they were on fire. And she'd never been so satisfied in her life.

"Lolly-girl? Are you still breathing?"

Grace could hear the humor and satisfaction in Toffer's voice.

"Yes, Master. Thank you so much."

"Just a taste of what's to come. Sleep well, little Lolly."

"But what about you?"

"Don't worry about me. Worry about doing as you're told. Goodnight, Lolly."

"Goodnight, Master."

The phone line went dead and Grace smiled. She felt needed, wanted, and loved. It was almost as if the entire day of accusations had never happened. Almost.

Chapter Seven

Note to self: You can teach your students best by having faith in yourself, and not letting false statements get you down.

To Do List:
Meet with Frank Medina and Watson after school
Try and write more on novel
Try not to let your students see how upset you are
Try and concentrate on work

Grace stared at her planner. Her note said to believe in herself, yet since the accusations of blackmail had surfaced, her To Do List had changed from do to try. She took a calming breath and looked around the room. Her students were deep into a pop quiz on *Julius Caesar* and the room was eerily quiet.

She'd been very careful with what she said to students, and very careful to make sure an adult office aide was present when she met with a student privately. That way no accusations could come up.

Her only real pleasures came from her daily phone calls with Toffer. She'd been very impressed that he started each conversation by asking how she was feeling, and what had happened that day. He'd encouraged her to get a lawyer, and she'd followed his advice.

Preston Stewart worked for the state teachers' association, and had been very helpful in guiding Grace through the ins and outs of what could, and probably would, happen.

"If they decide to hold an official investigation, don't be surprised if they suspend you during that time," Preston had said on Friday when she'd talked to him. "It's standard procedure. It will probably be with pay, so you shouldn't have to worry about that."

Grace bit her lip as she thought about being suspended. She'd been teaching for more than fifteen years and nothing like this had ever happened to her. It made her sick to her stomach to think about it.

It was now Monday, and she was scheduled to meet with Medina and Watson after school. And she had a feeling that the meeting would not be pleasant. She thought back to her time with Master last night. She loved their sessions, and the wonderful feelings, both physical and mental, that she felt.

They'd played with most of the toys in her box, except for the clit clamp. Master told her he wanted to see her face the first time it was attached, wanted to guide her through it and be there to experience it with her physically.

She turned her attention back to her students and tried not to worry about the meeting. Ten minutes before the end of the school day, Preston arrived at her classroom door. He smiled and nodded to students, and when they were gone he gave Grace pointers on how to act.

"Don't lose your temper," he said. "That would be the worst thing that could happen. Let me do the talking. Don't accuse Watson of sexual harassment. If it comes down to a hearing, I will bring that up at the proper time. I've already alluded to it in my letters to Medina and the board, so it won't be out of left field. The most important thing today is keeping your cool."

Grace repeated the mantra to herself as they made their way to Watson's office, exchanged greetings, and sat down. Her hands were clammy and she grasped them together in her lap.

"I think we should get straight to the point," Medina said. "Grace, you've given years of service to this school. But in light of the allegations of the two students involved, we feel an investigation is warranted. We believe this probe will be in the best interests of all involved. It will clear up the matter, totally, no matter what the outcome."

Grace tightened her clasped hands and bit her lip.

"How long do you expect this investigation to take?" Grace marveled at Preston's calm voice.

"A week or so," Media replied. "We will take official depositions from everyone involved, starting with Grace, tomorrow, if that will give you time to get ready."

"That's good for us," Preston said. "We don't need time to prepare, because we have nothing to hide. Ms. Kinison will tell the truth about events."

"We will schedule the official hearing two weeks from tomorrow night," Medina said.

"Valentine's Day." Grace's voice was flat.

"Yes, Valentine's Day," Medina said. "In between now and then, you will be suspended, with pay."

"I was already scheduled to be off three days next week," Grace said.

Medina informed her that the office would change her time off from personal time to suspension, so that Grace could keep her time off. Then they agreed to meet at Preston's office at nine the next morning.

Preston accompanied Grace while she went to the office to make sure her lesson plans were up-to-date. The office workers were sympathetic, but cautious. It wasn't until they got to her room to pick up her personal items that the tears she'd been holding back began to flow. Rebecca was sitting behind her desk, waiting to hear what had happened.

"I answered your phone," she said as she hugged Grace. "Toffer's called three times."

Grace nodded as she cried into her friend's shoulder, with Preston patting her back gently.

"I'm sure they'll want to depose you, too, Rebecca."

Becca nodded at the lawyer and then the phone rang. Grace looked at Toffer's number on the ID, and tried to steady her voice when she said hello. After she'd told him what happened, he asked to speak with Preston. They talked for a few minutes, while Becca tried to comfort Grace.

When she took the phone back, she could hear the anger in his voice. "Go out to dinner with Becca and Preston. Enjoy yourself and try to relax. Call me when you get home. And don't worry, Lolly, everything's going to be fine. I promise."

Dinner passed in a blur, and when Grace finally called Toffer at ten that evening, she had resigned herself to the fact that she would probably lose her job. Even if she was found innocent of all charges, which Preston assured her she would be, things would never be the same for her in the classroom. She could swallow the pill a little better if she'd heard back for one of the publishers she'd sent her work to, but she hadn't.

Toffer answered on the first ring.

"You're early," he said. "I didn't expect to hear from you until eleven or so."

"I just walked in the door."

"Does that mean you haven't stood in the corner, yet?"

Toffer's "tut-tut-tut" followed Grace's answer of no.

"Do it now. It will help you focus on getting into your Lolly-mode."

Grace quickly stripped and stepped into the now familiar corner.

"Don't you feel better already?"

"Yes, Master."

"Good. I'm sorry about your bad day, baby. But this Preston guy sounds like he knows what he's doing. He'll prove you innocent in no time."

"Thank you, Master. I'm trying to stay positive."

"You'll be too busy once you get here to think about much. You'll be getting ready for the party, and, of course, serving me."

Grace laughed. "That's almost a whole week. I don't get into L.A. until a week from Wednesday."

"Actually, your plane leaves Denver International at four tomorrow afternoon. Preston assured me that you would be done with your deposition by then, and he would drive you to the airport."

"Toffer, I can't leave here now."

"I'm going to ignore that little slip of the tongue, Lolly, and yes, you can. Preston says that once you're deposed, they won't want to talk to you. You can't sit in on the other depositions, so all you'd have to do is sit at home until you left for here. I just pushed it up a week or so. It will give us time to play."

"But if he needs to talk to me…"

"He can call you here. I've already given him the number. Make sure you pack tonight. I think your twenty minutes are up. Go and get on the bed, on all fours."

Grace's heart was pounding. Tomorrow. She was going to come face to face with her Master tomorrow. For the first time that day, a genuine smile appeared on her face. She put the phone on speaker and knelt on the bed.

"You know what I'm thinking about right now, Grace?"

"What?"

"Spanking your pretty little ass; taking you to dinner with no panties on and watching you squirm in your seat; and watching you moan when I attach the clamp to your clitty."

"Master."

"You won't have time to think about your problems, Grace, because I'm going to keep you very busy. I've got lots of fun games planned for you. Now, I want you to listen carefully to what you need to do when you get here tomorrow. There will be a driver to meet you at the airport. The minute you get into the limo, you belong to me, lock, stock and barrel. Understand?

"Wear a skirt on the plane. When you get into the car take off your panties, and then call me. Make sure the privacy shield is raised. Then, when you get to the house..."

Grace fought to keep her hands away from her dripping pussy as Master gave his instructions. An orgasm would help relieve the tension from the day. She could concentrate on pleasure, not on the problems caused by angry students and Joe Watson.

"Are you listening to me, Grace?"

"I'm sorry. My mind was wandering."

"I thought so. I hope you heard enough to know what to do, because I don't plan on repeating myself. And if you fail to follow my instructions to the letter, you will receive a pretty harsh punishment. As it is, you'll go without an orgasm tonight as punishment for not listening to me fully."

"Master, please. I'm so wet right now."

"No, Grace. The next time you come you'll be in my presence."

"I need to come. Master, *please*, I'm begging you."

"I know it's been a bad day, Lolly. But this will help you focus on tomorrow. Think about your pussy and how it's going to please me. Needing to have an orgasm, and being denied, will help you think about something other than your suspension. Take care, Gracie. I'll see you tomorrow night. Don't forget to pack all your new toys."

"Yes, Sir."

"Sleep well, little one."

The phone went dead and Grace collapsed onto the bed. Sleep well? When she needed to come after such a horrible day? How could she think about anything but the horrible thing that was taking place in her life?

Part way through her packing, she knew that Toffer had made a wise decision. For the last hour, all she'd thought about was Toffer and the week and a half they would spend together before Lindsey's party. She hadn't thought once about Dominic, or Joe Watson.

Her life wasn't all horrible right now. Toffer was a wonderful addition that had brought her new experiences, and promised to take her to new heights.

Her pussy, now used to nightly attention, ached for release. Grace kept her fingers to herself as she wrapped her toys in her clothing and placed them in her bag, praying that her luggage wouldn't be searched at the airport, and then laughing as she thought about the look on the security officer's face if it was.

Chapter Eight

Note to self: Thank Master for knowing exactly what to do, and for taking care of all the details so well.

To Do List:
Give deposition
Don't forget to pack laptop
Tell landlord about extended absence
Stop mail delivery
Call Becca and ask her to water plants
Try and recall exactly what you are supposed to do when you get to Master's house

The leather of the limo seat was cold against Grace's behind. The driver had been polite and efficient as he collected Grace and her luggage and loaded them both into the limo. While he put the luggage in the trunk, Grace took advantage of the privacy and shimmied out of her panties.

It had been a long morning. Her deposition had gone well, and she'd been happy that, other than the clerks, the only people there were herself, Preston, Frank Medina, and the school's lawyer, an older man named Carlton Bunch, who was polite and well-organized.

His questions had been succinct and kept on point. The only painful questions were about Watson, and his repeated advances toward her. Bunch suggested that she was making the whole thing up. Grace said Watson's advances were numerous, and made her very uncomfortable. She hadn't reported them earlier, because she'd wanted to handle it by herself.

She tried to refocus her mind as the car pulled into L.A. traffic. Grace had never been very thrilled about being in L.A. The crowds and smog had always dampened the charm of the city to her. She knew that Peter and Lindsey lived in Brentwood, and assumed that Toffer did, also. But she didn't know enough about L.A. geography to decide which direction they were heading.

While the car made its way onto the freeway, Grace dialed Toffer's cell number.

"How was your flight, Lolly?"

His pet name for her brought a smile to her face. "Fine. No turbulence and it was on time."

"Good. And is the leather cold against your behind?"

"Yes, Master."

"Tweak your clitty for me, just enough to make you hum for me."

Grace spread her legs, resting her head against the leather of the limo seat. How was it that yesterday she'd been sure that life was over, and right now she felt as if it was just beginning? She rubbed her clit and moaned out Toffer's name.

"I hope you remember what you're supposed to do."

"Could we clear up a point or two up? I know that..."

"Missed instructions bring punishments, so you need to learn to listen better. I'll be home around eight and I'll see you then. I'm so very glad that you're here, Lolly."

The phone went dead and Grace frowned. He had a habit of doing that, giving instructions and saying things before hanging up without a response. She pulled her fingers out from between her legs and watched as the city sped by. Well, sped by was overstating it. The traffic made it seem like it was crawling by.

Was this really happening? Was she going to spend a week and a half with a man she'd only met on the phone and over the internet? Was she really going to give him total control over her body? It was a fantasy come true, but Grace knew that if Toffer wasn't friends with Peter, she wouldn't be here.

She hadn't told Peter and Lindsey about the suspension. She didn't want to ruin Lindsey's party. After it was over, she would tell them what was going on. At least in her public life. Would she tell them about her relationship with Toffer? She doubted it. Nothing would probably come from this. How could it? He lived in L.A., which Grace detested, and she lived in Boulder. But if she lost her job, she wouldn't have a reason to stay in Boulder. Still, Grace doubted that she could ever live in California. It was way too crowded.

An hour and a half later, the car turned into a lavish neighborhood and Grace scooted across the seat to look at the houses. This wasn't the Brentwood area that she remembered from her last visit. She frowned as she tried to figure out which button to push to lower the privacy screen.

"Where are we?"

"On our way to Mr. Shelley's house."

"Does he not live in Brentwood?"

The driver's laugh sounded more like a snort. "No, ma'am. He lives in the Hills."

"And the Hills are, what?" Alive with the sound of music?

"A very affluent residential area, ma'am. Mr. Shelley's house is an architectural marvel, four stories that sits on four acres of land. Lots of steel and glass, with two swimming pools. You're going to love it."

The calm feeling that had built in Grace's stomach went south. Four stories? Two swimming pools? He'd told her that he was forty-three years old. What sort of forty-three year old writer could afford a house in the Hollywood Hills with four stories and two swimming pools?

If she asked the driver about Toffer, the man would probably think he had the wrong person in his car. Something told her, however, that Toffer Shelley was more than he'd made himself out to be. From what'd he'd said, she knew that he worked at the studio. But she thought he was a writer. He must be a big shot to be able to afford a house that large, and in this area.

He'd given her permission to explore the house until the housekeeper left at seven. She would try and figure out then what his job was, because she doubted that he wrote scripts with Peter and Lindsey.

The limo stopped at a gate, which the driver opened with a code. When the car started its windy ascent, Grace marveled at the scenery. The lush foliage molded itself against the driveway and hid all but the top level of the house from view. She could see floor to ceiling windows, surrounded by steel beams. A deck looked to wrap around the entire building on the top level.

And if Grace thought that little peek prepared her for the rest of the house, she was wrong. When the car stopped next to the house, Grace thought her jaw would drop off. This house wasn't a house. It was a palace. A woman in her mid-forties was bounding down the stairs with a man about the same age on her heels.

"Welcome, welcome," she said as she opened the door. "I'm Millie, Toffer's housekeeper and this is my husband, Rafe. He's the main groundskeeper. We're so happy to see Toffer have guests, especially a beautiful woman like yourself."

Grace smiled and tried to get a word in edgewise as Millie propelled her toward the stairs. Her husband and the limo driver, who finally identified himself as Steve, lifted her luggage from the trunk.

"Now, you have the full run of the house and Toffer told me to unpack your luggage in his room." Millie gave her a knowing wink and Grace blushed. "He won't be home until eight or so and we leave around seven. I've made a salad for dinner and it's chilling in the fridge. Now, let me show you around."

Grace stopped in the entryway and stared. The house had a homey feeling, even though it was decorated to the nines.

"The first two floors are mainly for show," Millie said. "Two living rooms, a den and two bathrooms on this first floor. The second floor has two guest bedrooms, two bathrooms, a living area and the dining room."

"Now the top two floors are where most of the actual "living" is done. The third floor has the kitchen, the den, the library, the theater room, and another bedroom and bathroom, and Toffer's work-out room. The top floor is Toffer's bedroom and bath."

Grace turned her stunned gaze away from the glass-enclosed room.

"An entire floor for his bedroom?"

Millie laughed. "Yup. The top floor is huge, the bedroom and baths take up most of the space. There are two baths, his and hers, on either side of the bedroom. A small staircase leads to an enclosed room that no one goes in but Toffer. The previous owners used it as a work-out room, but Toffer calls it his private sanctuary. He doesn't even let me clean it, and it's the only room in the house that's not totally open with windows."

Grace nodded and surveyed the living area on the bottom floor again. She knew what was in the "private sanctuary." Toffer had told her that he's set up a mini-dungeon in there, and that he was looking forward to showing her around it, and trying out his new toys on her.

"Now, there are staircases at the front of the house, and another set in the back. There are decks on each level so you can enjoy the view. One swimming pool is further down the property, and one nearer the house. And there is a dumb-waiter system to move things from one floor to another. I'll show you how it works."

"No elevator?" Grace laughed.

"Of course there is," Millie said with a grin. "But we don't ever use it."

She guided Grace through each room, stopping to point out different works of art, or views of star's houses. When they finally reached the fourth floor Grace, who thought she was prepared for anything, stopped short. The room was huge. Against a large bank of windows rested a bed that looked to be more than a king. It was covered in a black quilted bedspread, with more than eight pillows lined up to the edges and on top of each other. The his and hers bathrooms were also decorated in black, this time in marble and chrome. And off to the end, against a wall filled with a flat-screen TV and shelves stuffed with DVDs was the staircase that led to the dungeon.

Grace gulped as she thought about what she would be doing in that room.

"This is unbelievable. I never expected something so spectacular."

"Mr. Shelley likes his privacy," Millie said. "Although this whole house is full of glass, there is hardly space outside for the, um, well, for anyone to look in. And the curtains in this room are mechanical and cover the entire side. There's a control for them on both nightstands. Now, you just make yourself at home and, if you need anything, there is an intercom system on the nightstand."

Grace had turned down Millie's offer to unpack her suitcases, not wanting the housekeeper to see her toys. After being shown where to put things in "her" bathroom, Grace unpacked quickly, tucking the sex toys into the nightstand drawer nearer the sliding glass doors. She figured that would be "her" side of the bed since the drawer was empty.

Or would it be? Grace had read about some Masters who had their submissives sleep on the floor next to the bed, or in another room entirely. Since her trip to California had literally happened overnight, the sleeping arrangements hadn't been discussed. Although Toffer had told Millie that he and Grace would be sharing his bedroom.

She crossed to the sliding glass doors and opened it to the warm California sun. Even though it was February it was still beautiful outside. Too cold, though, for a swim. She went onto the deck and smiled at the hot tub that took up the far wall. Too cold to swim, but not to soak.

A glance at her watch showed her that she had a half-hour before Millie and Rafe left, and she had to prepare for Master's arrival. She racked her brain to make sure she had the right instructions. Crossing to her bathroom she looked around until she saw the box sitting on the dresser. She'd overlooked it earlier.

She opened the carton, shivers running up and down her spine as she took out wrist and ankle cuffs. A blindfold rested under the cuffs. She was to bathe, and put on the cuffs, and then what? Wait downstairs? No, that wasn't right. She was to wait up here. Master had said he'd honk the horn when he arrived, and at that point she was to put on the blindfold and wait.

Was she supposed to kneel? Or stand? She couldn't remember. She would kneel. That was the most submissive position known to man, right? That's what she would do. She just hoped that she did the right thing.

She put the cuffs back into the box and went downstairs. On the third floor she found the library, which had obviously been a bedroom before Toffer had converted it. The wall to ceiling shelves were lined with fiction books, both modern and classic and Grace smiled. Two large reclining chairs sat with a round table in the middle. Perfect for a couple.

She explored the other rooms, laughing at pictures that she found of Peter and Lindsey. Mixed in with those were pictures of Peter and Drake Dawson laughing and drinking a beer on the deck of this house.

Grace stared at the wall of photos. There seemed to be a lot of photos of Drake Dawson. Grace shook her head and wondered which of these men in the group photos was Toffer. No matter how hard she tried, her mind kept wandering back to the pictures of the handsome actor, and she wondered how close he and Toffer were. The pictures showed Drake with many different Hollywood stars and starlets, and Grace thought it was strange for Toffer to have so many photos of the man in his house.

Was Toffer bi? Did he and Drake Dawson have a relationship and that's why there were so many pictures of the actor around? It could be, Grace realized. It wasn't unheard of for a bi-man, or a bi-woman, to want a relationship with a person of the opposite sex. Toffer hadn't mentioned anything about it but the idea had merit. And if they had a relationship, would he share her with Drake? The idea made her shiver. Drake Dawson was the most sought-after bachelor in Hollywood. She was sure that he wouldn't look twice at her. And if he was bi, then it was a well-hidden secret.

At seven on the dot, Millie informed Grace that she and her husband were leaving.

"We've already locked up and we don't usually come in until around ten in the morning, so we'll see you then. Have a good time!" Millie winked at her and Rafe laughed.

When they were gone, Grace walked the three flights of stairs to Toffer's bedroom. She stripped and took a long soak in a bubble bath. It felt wonderful to be so far away from the worries of her suspension and the lies about her accepting bribes. She dried off and liberally applied lotion to her entire body. Her fingers shook as she fastened the wrist and ankle cuffs. A look at the clock showed that she had fifteen minutes before Toffer was due home.

Her heart was already beating a mile a minute. When he got here, she was sure it would fall out of her chest and bounce around on the floor. She wrapped herself in a large terrycloth robe and walked out on the deck. In the darkness, the lights of Los Angeles looked beautiful. She leaned on the railing and closed her eyes.

How had something this wonderful happened to her, Grace Kinison, school teacher and wanna-be writer? She allowed her mind to wander to the idea that she and Toffer were married and that this house was hers, that she actually lived here instead of just visiting. She was so far gone in her thoughts that when the horn sounded she jumped.

He was here. He was here. Oh lord, what was she supposed to do? The blindfold. Grace ran back inside, paused to close the curtains, and ran into the bathroom to grab the blindfold. She could hear his footsteps on the stairs as she fastened it over her eyes and knelt in front of the bed.

Wait, wait, this wasn't right. She was supposed to be on the bed. That's what it was. She dropped the robe on a chair and scrambled onto the soft comforter, knelt with her legs spread and her ass to the room and clasped her hands behind her back. She turned her head to rest it against the mattress.

"You were listening. Very good, Lolly-girl."

"Thank you, Master."

Grace tried to get a handle on her breathing. It wouldn't do for him to have to call rescue because she'd passed out. She could hear him moving around behind her, the clink of keys catching her attention.

"You're as beautiful as I thought you'd be," Toffer said. He molded each ass cheek with a hand and gently kneaded her soft skin. Grace bit her lip to keep from crying out in pleasure as his fingers moved down to explore her wet folds.

"Thank you, again, Master."

"I've been hard all day just thinking about this. I was going to punish you first, for all those times you forgot and called me Toffer. Lay my flogger across your ass until you begged for mercy. But now, I think I just have to fuck you first. Would you like that, Lolly?"

"Yes, Master."

Her heart was beating wildly. This was really happening. She was being submissive. She was calling a man Master.

"No more talking without permission, unless you're answering a question. Stand up, Lolly." Grace was grateful for Toffer's help as she stood, her arms still clasped behind her back. She bit back a gasp as Master locked the wrist cuffs together.

When he knelt behind her and she felt cold metal against her legs, she gasped.

"Easy, Lolly. It's just a spreader bar, to keep you open for me. Move your legs a little farther apart."

Grace almost lost her balance when she moved. Master put his arm around her to steady her, and then used both hands to lock the bar into place on the ankle cuffs.

"There we go. All trussed up for me." He ran his hands up and down her sides, and then caressed her breasts, twisting and pulling on her nipples, until Grace thought she would scream out for him to fuck her.

She felt very vulnerable. And very sexy. When his fingers began to explore her pussy, Grace whimpered. His index finger traced a path from her opening to her clit and back before pushing inside. Grace fought to stay upright. He was exploring, and she was dying.

"Please." The word came out before she could stop it and he answered with a sharp slap to her ass.

"Master, I…" Another sharp slap to the other ass cheek caused her to gasp. Then two more landed on each buttock. Without saying anything, or admonishing her for breaking the rules, Master went back to feeling her folds. She wished he would say something. The silence was making her nervous.

His hands were gentle as he explored and Grace relaxed into the spreader bar, getting used to the feeling of standing with her legs so far apart. When he pinched her clit, she gasped and her knees gave out, and she was thankful that he reached out to steady her.

Master pinched it again and again and again as she bucked into his hands. She could feel an orgasm building. Just a few more pinches was all it would take.

"Hold still," he said sharply, as he slapped her ass again. "And don't you dare come, not until I give you permission. You know that rule."

It wasn't a question, per se, but Grace still felt the need to answer.

"Yes, Master."

"Good girl."

He stood and pulled her into him, his hard cock pushing against her ass. He put his fingers, dripping with her wetness on her lips.

"Taste."

Grace bit down the urge to say, "hell, no," before she began licking his fingers as he murmured his approval in her ear.

"I'm going to fuck you now, Lolly. I'm going to help you kneel on the bed. When you're there and you feel me kneeling behind you, the order not to speak is rescinded until we are done. Do you understand?"

"Yes, Master."

Grace felt as if she was moving in baby steps as Master turned her toward the bed and helped her kneel, positioning her so that he could mount her. When her nipples rubbed against the spread she moaned. How in the world was she going to keep from coming before Master told her she could?

* * *

Toffer stepped back and looked at his beautiful submissive. She was more perfect than he could ever have imagined. So beautiful, so plush and soft, so willing. He caressed her thighs and smiled as he watched her bite her lip to keep from crying out.

He quickly shed his clothes and retrieved a condom from the nightstand. His cock had been rock hard all day and he didn't know how long he was going to last. When it was over, after he'd claimed her in the most primitive of ways, he'd show her that he was Drake Dawson. He'd worried about her reaction all day. He should have told her at some point, but Toffer was having too much fun playing. It was a fantastic feeling to have a woman want him as Toffer. Drake got his share of hotties, but after a while, he wondered if the women were attracted to the man, or the name. With Grace, he knew that she wanted him for himself.

Besides, in this house he was Toffer. He'd made sure Steve, Millie, and Rafe knew not to refer to him as Drake in front of Grace.

He knelt behind her, putting his legs on either side of hers, the spreader bar still in place. He wanted her to get used to the bar because he planned on using it a lot. It was his favorite bondage apparatus, keeping a submissive very vulnerable and in position to be fucked, either in front or back, whenever he wanted.

"Do you want my cock, Lolly?"

"Yes, Master."

"Louder. Tell me where you want it."

"I want your cock in my pussy, Master. Please."

"Beg me."

Toffer bit his lip. Beg me? Crap, at this point, he would beg her.

"Please, Master, please. Fuck me."

"You're not convincing me."

"Please." She drew the word out and bucked her hips toward him as he sheathed his cock in the condom.

"Master, please. I'll be good. I need you. I want you. Please fuck me!" She punctuated her words with hard thrusts as she fought to break free of the bar and cuffs and she yelled "please," over and over again.

Toffer pulled her head up until his mouth was on her ear. He could feel her shivering beneath him and he knew that all it would take was one little pull on her clit, one long thrust of his cock and she would come.

"You belong to me now. All of you. Every last inch. Your pussy. Your ass. Your mouth. Your tits. They're all mine." And he plunged inside her. He felt her orgasm spread through her body as she screamed out, "Master," her pussy clenching him like a vise.

When her muscles relaxed, he pushed her hips down and rode her, slamming in and out of her.

"You're a bad girl, Lolly. You came without permission. That means you'll meet the flogger tonight, after all. And it'll be much harder than the spanking I made you give yourself."

Her whimpers were more sighs of delight as he continued to fuck her. God. He'd never been inside a woman as tight and warm and welcoming as Grace. He'd never felt more at home inside a woman than he did inside Grace's pussy.

"Who do you belong to?" His thrusts increased as his orgasm neared.

"I'm yours, Master. All of me. Fuck me, make me yours."

Toffer collapsed on top of her, the cuffs and spreader bar pushing into him as he pounded out his orgasm. When he finally steadied himself on shaking hands and knees he whispered, "Did I hurt you, Lolly-girl?"

"No, Master." Her words were soft. He stood and walked to the bathroom to discard the condom. He looked in the mirror and took a deep breath. It was time to face the music.

Once in the bedroom, he looked at the bound woman on his bed. He could see wetness against her thighs and his cock twitched. Damn, how did she do that? He'd just come and he was ready for more. He helped Grace to stand. Then he kissed her gently, his mouth becoming more and more demanding as their lips danced together. After a few minutes he gently caressed her cheeks.

"Close your eyes and keep them closed until I say so."

The blindfold came off easily and Toffer kissed each eyelid. "Open."

He stepped back and watched as she became accustomed to being able to see again. Then her eyes widened and her mouth opened.

"No, no. It can't be."

"Yes, Grace." He grabbed her as she tried to hobble away.

"You lied to me! Pig! Jerk! Let me go! Oh my god!" Tears were streaming down her face.

Toffer turned her and slapped her ass repeatedly. "Is that any way to speak to your Master?"

"Is this some sort of joke you two play? Let me go!"

Toffer pushed her back onto the bed. She came to rest on her bound hands and he moved her so that she was lying on her side.

"I'm Toffer Shelly, Grace. That's my birth name. I'm the man you've talked to all this time. I'm your Master. Take deep breaths and relax. Deep breaths."

"Get away from me! Don't touch me. Let me go, now!"

Grace struggled to get away from him, inching as far as her binding would allow.

"I want you to calm down. Stop it right now."

Tears of anger streaked her face and Toffer felt sick to his stomach. He'd underestimated how this would affect her. He'd brought her to the height of pleasure, and then pulled her into a hole, one that she was already part of, thanks to that asshole Joe Watson.

He retrieved his wallet and stretched out next to her. "Look at my driver's license. Christopher Shelley, next to my picture. I'm not lying to you, Grace. I want you to listen to me and hear my reasons for this. This doesn't change anything between us."

"No, Toffer, it changes everything."

Chapter Nine

Note to self: What good are self-improvement notes when you keep getting screwed at all ends?

To Do List:
Fly back to Boulder
Call Peter and curse him out
Call Becca to pick me up at the airport
Try and forget about the fantastic orgasm you had at the hands of Drake Dawson

Grace wiped her eyes and reviewed what she'd just written. Drake Dawson. Drake Dawson. She'd had sex with Drake Dawson. She'd been naked in his room. He'd bound her. His cock had been inside her. She'd called him Master.

She slammed her head back into the pillow in his guest bedroom. How in the hell had this happened? She felt humiliated. The perfect Drake Dawson, who could have any woman in the world, used her for sex. She was sure that it would make for interesting talk at the studio the next day: *Hey, I tricked this voluptuous chick into calling me Master. She let me tie her up. She begged me for it. It was cool.*

She closed her eyes and his face appeared before her, his words echoed in her ears.

"Hear me out."

"Untie me! Now!"

"I just wanted you to want me as Toffer, not as Drake. Shit, you have no idea how hard it is to be judged by your looks."

"Are you kidding me? Look at me!" Grace had tried to sit up, then fallen back when the spreader bar kept her from gaining her feet. "You don't think people judge me by my looks? They judge me because I'm not perfect, because I'm fat! And did I lie to you? *No!* I sent you a picture. You *bastard!*"

She'd started crying uncontrollably, barely noticing as he unlocked the cuffs and pulled the spreader bar out from between her ankles. He'd tried to pull her into his arms and she'd pushed him away, running into the "her" bathroom and grabbing the robe she'd worn earlier before flying down the stairs to the spare bedroom.

He hadn't tried to follow her, and she'd thrown herself on the bed, crying in anger until she'd fallen asleep. When she'd woken up an hour later, her head was pounding. Her suitcases and clothes were arranged neatly on the dresser, her laptop and briefcase sat on the desk.

A look at the clock told her that three hours had passed since their fight. It was a little after two. She wondered if he was sleeping. Mentally, she kicked herself for overreacting. According to his license, he really was Toffer Shelley. He was right. He hadn't lied to her. He just hadn't told her the exact truth.

And truthfully, she could blame herself for it, too. She hadn't asked him what he did for a living. If she had, would he have lied to her? Or would he have told her the truth? There was no way to tell now. But this was the man who had guided her through many things in the past few weeks, including the horror that was ruining her career.

He'd pushed her toward higher levels of sexual pleasure, and laughed at her jokes, encouraged her to write and given her a shoulder to cry on.

Whether he was Toffer Shelley or Drake Dawson, he was a wonderful man who had comforted her when disaster had struck. She wrapped the robe around her and padded up the stairs. The door to his room was open, and a faint light filled the bedroom.

"Toffer?"

"Over here."

He was sitting in a chair on the deck, drinking a beer.

"I'm sorry. I overreacted."

"No, baby, I'm sorry. It was wrong of me not to tell you the truth. A BDSM relationship is supposed to be built on trust. I broke that trust."

"Not really. I can see your point. I never thought about someone judging a good-looking person just by their looks. People must bug you all the time."

Toffer laughed, and then shook his head. "I can find you a hotel tomorrow, my treat. Or I'll fly you back to Boulder, and then back here for the party."

"Are those my only options?" She waited a beat, and added, "Master?"

Grace bit her lip, and then backed away from the light. She knew that her eyes would be puffy from crying, her face blotchy.

"Kneel before me, Lolly." His voice was low.

Grace dropped the robe and sank to her knees. She pressed her face into his palm when he took her face in his hands.

"Do you still want to submit to me?"

"Yes, Master."

"Are you positive?"

"Absolutely."

He pulled her forward, leaned down and kissed her forehead.

"Do I get to meet the flogger tonight?"

Toffer's laugh filled the quiet night air.

"Not tonight. Tonight, or should I say, this morning, I just want us to sleep together. That will help heal your wounds, bring us closer. Tonight, when I get home I'll introduce you to the flogger."

* * *

Note to self: Try to control your outbursts better. Get all the facts before you judge, and learn not to judge so easily.

To Do List:

Work on novel

Call Peter and see where he is with the party planning

Remember every wonderful moment of the fantastic orgasm you had at the hands of Drake Dawson, scratch that, Toffer Shelley, and the wonderful time you spent sleeping in his arms

Grace looked over her revised To Do list. She'd slept late that morning, cozily burrowing into the sheets after Toffer had kissed her lightly at five and said he'd be home around eight. He hadn't touched her again last night, except to pull her close to him while they slept. It had been so long since Grace had slept next to a man that she'd lain away for a long time, listening to the beating of his heart near her ears. It was a fantastic feeling that fueled her for the day.

For lunch, she and Millie had eaten the Cobb salad from last night, after the housekeeper had made sly comments about the couple not eating last night.

She planned on writing all afternoon, but first she wanted to check her e-mail. There was one from Preston, who said things were fine. Depositions were going well and he'd found proof that Dominic and his father had met with Watson a week before the accusations were made.

There was one from Peter telling her that he knew she was at Toffer's house, and that a party planner was picking up most of what needed to be done. The woman might have a few questions for Grace about photos and stories and if she did, she would contact her through e-mail.

"Have fun with Toffer. He told me about what happened with you."

Grace stared at the words. Had Toffer told Peter that she was allowing the actor to dominate her? She doubted it. Peter had probably received a watered down version about how Grace didn't know about Toffer's professional persona, and how angry she'd been. She finished reading the e-mail.

"Don't be angry with him. He's a great guy and it's hard on him to get to know people. I think he really does have a thing for you."

The words made Grace blush. She was just about to close out the e-mail program and get down to work when a ding told her that a new message had arrived. She recognized Toffer's address and opened the file.

Inside were explicit instructions about how she was to be attired, and in what position she was supposed to be in, when he arrived home that evening. The ending sent her into full body shivers.

"It's time for you to act on your new name."

Lolly-girl. *I want to lick you like a lollipop.* Eight o'clock couldn't come fast enough.

* * *

Toffer turned off the engine of his jeep and ran his fingers through his dark hair. It had been a long day. They'd had to re-shoot scenes and tempers were flaring because work on the episode wasn't going well. He would probably have to work late Thursday and Friday, and possibly work on Saturday, too.

The idea sucked because he didn't want to work. He wanted to spend time with Grace. His cock twitched as he thought of her upstairs in his bedroom, waiting for him. Totally naked except for the wrist, ankle cuffs and spreader bar.

The mental image of Grace gave him an instant erection. It was an incredible feeling, and helped to counteract the fight he'd had with Giselle that day. The model had been in his trailer at lunchtime, naked, and his cock hadn't reacted at all. The beautiful blond had massaged her breasts and begged him to fuck her.

"Please, Drake, nobody gives it to me like you do."

"No, Giselle, the Drake cock mobile is closed for you. We are finished. I thought you understood that."

She'd screamed in rage, thrown everything she could get her hands on and then dressed and stormed out. He hoped that was the last he'd see of her.

He went inside, checked the mail and messages and then slowly made his way upstairs. He stood in the doorway, staring at her as she lay spread-eagle on his bed. Her beautiful breasts caught his attention. He wanted to do everything at once, take the whole night and play. They could do it all, but then the anticipation of new things would be gone.

She'd been so damn tight last night, and she'd responded to being bound like he knew she would, with total abandon and enjoyment. For the millionth time that day, he thanked the stars that she'd forgiven him and come back to his bed last night.

"How was your day, Lolly?"

"Fine, Master. And yours?"

"It's better now. I see you mastered the process of attaching the spreader bar yourself. On your knees."

His hard cock pulsed as she dropped onto her knees, albeit a little clumsily, and clasped her hands behind her back.

"Did you play with your pussy, today?"

"No, Master."

"Good." He stood before her and pulled her face into his crotch. "Are you hungry for me?"

"Yes, Master."

"I like to hear that. But first I want to fill your ass."

He felt her stiffen and he smiled. "Not with my cock, not yet anyway."

Toffer walked to the nightstand and opened the drawer. He moved things around and then pulled out an anal plug.

"This one will do. It'll help to open you up for when I do fuck your ass. Bend over the bed."

* * *

The wonderful feeling of anticipation that had taken over Grace at seven o'clock intensified as she watched Toffer walk toward her with the plug in his hand. She'd never, ever, had anything inside her that way. The idea was intriguing. It was exciting. It was terrifying.

With Master's help, Grace stood and then bent over the bed. She felt totally vulnerable, but wasn't that what she wanted. She wanted to try the nasty things, under the guidance of her Master.

When Master pulled her cheeks apart, she flinched. No one had ever looked at her there unless he was a medical doctor. When his finger traced the rosette she pushed up on her toes in an effort to get away and he swatted her behind.

"Very fuckable." His words sang in her ears. "Relax, Lolly. We'll work this inside you and you'll wear it tonight. It'll be uncomfortable at first, but you'll get used to it. Tomorrow you'll wear one from noon until I get home."

Grace mentally calculated the time. That would make eight hours with a plug up her ass. She would have it there while she talked to Millie and Rafe. The idea thrilled her. She would be doing something very naughty for her Master and no one would know.

A cold cream touched her private spot, and she gasped when Master's finger slipped past the opening.

"Do you feel this, feel how I'm doing this? You need to pay attention for when you insert the plug tomorrow."

Do I ever! "Yes, Master."

"Makes sure you use enough cream tomorrow to ease the entry." He pushed his finger all the way in and Grace moaned when he moved it around, spreading the cream on her insides. When he left her, she sighed. The cream was reapplied and, this time, two fingers slipped inside. He lightly fucked her with them.

The sensation was incredible. She felt full, if a little uncomfortable. Her breath came out in tiny little gasps.

"You like having me invade you this way. Don't deny it; I can hear your little mews."

Grace nodded, and then moaned when Master slapped her ass.

"Never nod. Always answer me with words."

"Yes, Master."

"Spread your cheeks for me."

Grace followed his instructions. Her breathing increased as Master fucked her with his fingers for a few more minutes, and then quickly withdrew and placed the plug at her anus.

"Push out gently." When she did, the tip of the plug slipped inside her and a light burning sensation spread through her behind. Grace tried to push the intruder out.

"Stop, Lolly." He pushed the plug farther in and Grace tried to wiggle away.

"Too much, Master. Please."

Master held the plug still and Grace tried to get her breathing under control.

"Relax. You can do this. I want you to do this. Submit to me, Grace."

His words echoed in her ears. Grace exhaled and pulled her cheeks apart more. The plug moved deeper inside her and the original feeling of burning and being uncomfortable dissipated. It felt incredible. Master twisted the plug inside her and Grace bucked against him. It felt liberating.

When she sensed the edges of the plug against her backside, she knew that it was totally inside her.

"Just hold your cheeks apart so I can admire your full ass. Very nice, Lolly. Very well done. Tomorrow when you put it in, remember to use lots of lube. I'll leave a tube in your bathroom. Take it slow if you need to, but I want you to wear it from noon to eight. It doesn't come out until I get home. Understand?"

"Yes, Master."

"Good. Just stay there for a little bit. Hold very still and I'll be back later."

Grace could hear him moving around the room. The sound of his clothing coming off was followed by the sound of the shower turning on. The plug felt like it was expanding in her ass. The feeling of fullness was returned full-blown once the object was totally inside her. Although it was alien to her, she enjoyed the sensation. She wiggled her behind, and moved her pussy up and down on the spread. It felt so good.

More than the physical aspects, though, were the mental aspects. She loved the fact that she was doing this for Toffer, that he was getting pleasure out of seeing her naked and full.

The shower turned off and his whistling filled the air. He was moving around, doing things in the bathroom. What was taking so long? Her pussy had been wet since he'd inserted the plug, really since she'd attached the spreader bar, and she needed to play.

She wiggled her behind again, enjoying the feeling of the plug in her behind. When she moved this time, her pussy rubbed harder against the bedspread and sent tingles through her body. Damn, that felt good. She wiggled more and her clit, already on fire, tightened more. The crack of a towel against her buttocks shocked her back to the room.

"Hold still. Did I give you permission to do that? I seem to remember telling you to lie still."

"No, Master. I'm sorry, Master, I just need to..."

"You need to do as you're told, not give yourself pleasure. I say when you get pleasure and when you don't. Remember that your body belongs to me, now. When I tell you to lie still that's exactly what I mean. Well, you had a punishment coming anyway. I just guess I'll have to alter my plan and bring it on now. I don't like having to change my plans, Grace. You've been a bad girl. Hold very still."

Grace moaned as she felt him lock the wrist cuffs together. The sound of him going up the stairs made her smile. He was going to his little dungeon, but he wasn't taking her. She wanted to go, too. She was tempted to yell at him to take her with him. The knowledge of what was up there intrigued her.

He returned moments later, laying his body on top of hers so that the plug pushed in even more. He laid the flogger in front of her face and Grace closed her eyes. He was going to whip her.

"Kiss the handle. Kiss the leather. Show me you want to receive your punishment, that you're not being forced."

The leather was cold against her lips. She kissed the handle as he turned it around, then kissed the tips of the thongs.

He stood and ran the strands across her behind. "It's very important to me that you do this because you want to. That you trust me enough to know what to do. Do you trust me?"

"Yes, Master."

"Good girl. If at any point it becomes unbearable, you say Drake, and I'll stop. Understand?"

"Yes, Master." They'd talked about safe words during their e-mails and IMs. Still, that discussion hadn't prepared

Grace for the fact that she was about to be whipped. She was frightened, her stomach turning flip-flops over and over inside her.

"Relax, Gracie. This first one won't be hard. Just enough for you to get to know the sensation. Just enough for you to know that you need to obey the rules. But if you keep breaking the rules, the flogger may be replaced with the crop. Trust me when I say you don't want that to happen."

The traces of the leather on her behind didn't hurt and Grace relaxed somewhat. Moments later the flogger cracked through the air and came down on her behind. She tensed her muscles as the pain spread through her backside. The strands came down again and again and again.

"Master." Her behind felt like it was on fire. "Please, I'll be good."

"You do not have permission to speak." The leather came down again and again and Grace bit her lip to try and stay silent. It wasn't really painful. The initial sting hurt, and then the sting turned into a pleasure that tortured her already engorged clit.

When the straps moved down to the tender spot between her buttocks and legs she let out a cry of pain. They landed twice more in the same area and Grace thought she would come out of her skin. Now that hurt. Badly.

"Who do you belong to, Lolly?"

"You, Master."

He traced the leather across her backside. "Who makes the rules, and who follows them?"

"You make the rules, and I follow them."

"Good girl. Have I made my point?"

"Yes, Master."

"Shall I continue whipping you, or will you behave?"

"I'll behave, Master, I promise."

He draped himself over her body again, placing the leather near her lips.

"Kiss the flogger. Show me that you have learned from, and accepted, your punishment."

Grace traced her lips up and down the flogger's handle, trailing them over Master's hand as he held the object.

"Good girl. Now it's time for you to make good on your promise, Lolly-girl."

He quickly unlocked her cuffs, and pulled the spreader bar out from between her ankles. Then he sat in the middle of the bed and spread his legs. "Crawl to me, Grace."

The plug moved inside her as she crawled, her burning behind up in the air.

"Lick me like a lollipop. Don't suck, just lick."

Grace lowered her head and ran her tongue up his length. She hadn't realized last night how large he was. She'd just been thrilled to have him inside her. Now her tongue ran up and down him and she realized he was at least eight, maybe nine, inches long, and thick. How in the world was she going to take all this up her ass? The plug was becoming uncomfortable right now. What would it feel like when it was replaced by Master's cock?

She felt him shiver under her attention as she moved back and forth. Her tongue trailed to his balls and his shivering increased. He felt delicious under her tongue. When he threaded his hands in her hair and murmured her name, not Grace, but Lolly, she felt a wonderful stirring of belonging. He'd given her that name. Only him. She belonged to him.

"Suck me, Lolly. Take me inside you."

He filled her mouth totally as she slid up and down, lightly running her teeth up and down his length before pushing her lips over them so she could suck harder.

"Fuck, oh fuck, Lolly, baby."

He still had his hands in her hair, but he allowed her to set the pace. She could feel him growing, his cock twitching inside her mouth. She knew he was about to come and she remembered her promise to swallow it all. She'd never done that before, and she knew now that with Master she would do it over and over, but only with Master.

His growled, "Lolly-girl," signaled his orgasm, and seconds later his warm liquid filled her mouth. Grace sucked greedily, pushed on by his oft repeated, "Fuck, yes."

When she'd sucked him dry, she laid her head on his thigh.

"Play with your clit. Come for me."

Grace rose up, the plug sliding deeper inside her as she delved into her wetness. She was so turned on she knew it wouldn't take much to send her over the edge.

"Good girl. Come, come now." And she did. Her orgasm sent her tumbling into an abyss as Master stroked her hair and held her head against his thigh.

"My beautiful little Lolly. I'm so glad that you're mine."

Chapter Ten

Note to self: There is a world outside Toffer's house. Don't allow yourself to become too accustomed to this wonderful feeling. He's never mentioned anything about forever.

To Do List:

Finish last four chapters of novel

Answer Lindsey's e-mail and convince her that I'm all right

Return Becca's call with same message

Try to behave myself and not jump Master's bones when he comes home tonight

Grace was becoming accustomed to California. She'd been here for five days now and each day was an improvement over the last one. Even though it was February, it was beautiful outside. Not exactly hot, but it was in the seventies. And Becca had told her that it was snowing, again, in Boulder.

She knew that it wasn't just California she was enjoying. Her time with Toffer was wonderful. She clinched her muscles and smiled as the plug she was wearing moved inside her. Master required her to wear it for three hours each day. He said it gave him a silent thrill to know she was here obeying his wishes. And it gave her more than a silent thrill.

In the five days since she'd been submitting to Toffer, she'd had more orgasms than she'd had in her entire life. And in more varied ways. He still hadn't taken her to the dungeon. He said he was saving that for Sunday, when he had an entire day to "torture" her. He'd raised his eyebrows up and down and then laughed maniacally.

She read over her carefully worded e-mail to Lindsey, who was frantic about not being able to find her friend after she'd called the school and been told that Grace was on suspension.

The subject line had screamed, "WHERE THE HELL ARE YOU!" and Grace had winced. It was unfair of her not to have told Lindsey what was happening. Even though her friend was very busy, Grace knew she would try and contact her at some point. She felt horrible that she hadn't been there to answer the phone, or to offer assurances that things were fine.

In her answer, she'd explained the problem, and said that she was staying in Denver with friends. She hated lying to her, but if she told the truth then Lindsey was liable to find about the party, and Peter would kill Grace.

"I'm fine, really." More than fine. "Don't worry about me, because I'm beginning to think this is for the best." *My writing has never been better.* "And I think I might have sold a story."

Grace clicked on the letter from the online publisher expressing interest in a short story and asking to see more of her work. She couldn't wait to show it to Toffer tonight. She'd already shared it with Millie, who offered to cook a special dinner for the two of them to celebrate.

When the e-mail was sent, Grace opened her short stories file to try and decide what to send to the publisher. She was deep into reading a story she'd written several years ago, when a woman's voice sounded from the door of the library.

"Does Drake know what you do all day, what he's paying you for?"

Grace looked up to see an absolutely stunning woman looking at her; anger blazed on her face.

"Excuse me?"

"Well, I guess you're the new housekeeper since the other fat one is gone."

A look at her watch showed that it was just after four. Millie had gone to the store to pick up steaks and a bottle of wine for dinner tonight.

"Who are you?"

"I'm Drake's girlfriend, Giselle." When Grace didn't respond, the woman huffed.

"The model? I don't have to clean someone else's house for a living like you obviously do. Although it doesn't look like you're doing more than sitting on your ass."

Grace straightened her back. "I'm not a maid. I'm Toffer's guest."

The woman laughed. "Toffer? He left that name behind long ago. If you're his 'guest,' you would know that."

"And if you're his 'girlfriend' I would have seen you before now, seeing as how I've been here for almost a week."

Grace could see the moment understanding dawned in the model. She'd obviously been ignored for a while, and now she knew why. She couldn't help feeling smug over the fact.

"I don't believe that he would dump me for your fat ass."

"I don't care what you believe," Grace said as she stood.

Giselle looked her up and down. "Well, maybe he wanted to play with your tits. But he'll tire of those before long. Other than your tits, you're much too fat for his tastes. Drake and I have been an item for years. I won't let you come between us, so I suggest you pack and leave."

"How did you get in here?" Millie's voice was harsh.

"Through the gate. I know the code, remember?"

"You need to leave."

"No. I plan on having a nice dinner with Drake. It's being delivered, so you can shove off. And you, *guest*, can just go to your room. You're not invited to this party."

"Well, since I'm staying in Toffer's room, I guess I'll just go up there. Millie, don't worry about cooking. Toffer and I will do it when he gets home. And you, *Giselle*, can be the one to shove off. Something tells me Toffer didn't invite you, and he won't be happy to find you here."

Grace picked up her laptop and left with her head held high. She knew that Toffer wanted her here. For five days, she had seen neither hide nor hair of this woman, not a toothbrush or a T-shirt. Toffer had never mentioned her and Grace trusted him implicitly. She was sure that if Giselle was here when Toffer got home that the fur was going to fly.

* * *

Toffer frowned at the myriad of cars in his driveway. Millie and Rafe were still here. There was a delivery van from a popular L.A. restaurant and beyond that… Shit. Giselle's car. Did the woman not take a hint? He'd told her they were done the other day. He mentally kicked himself. He hadn't, however, taken back the key or changed the code at the gate.

He walked inside of the house and stopped in the foyer. It was eerily silent. "Grace?"

"In here, Toffer." Her voice was low and sweet and he grinned. He found them all in the kitchen. Giselle was paying the delivery boy, an eager college student who was staring openly at the beautiful model. Grace was sitting at the bar, smiling, and Millie was biting her thumbnail. Rafe was standing guard in the doorway to the dining room.

"Darling!" Giselle's voice rang out as she ran to him. He caught her before she could fling herself at him and pushed her away.

"What are you doing here?"

"Well, I know we had a tiff, but I forgive you. Your *little* houseguest, however, is less than cordial. I told her that you would want to be alone with me, but…"

"Giselle, I don't want to be anywhere with you. I thought I made that clear. I want you to leave."

"Drake." She pushed her full lips into a pout. The delivery boy moaned out a "man, you're nuts," and Grace tried, and failed, to hide a laugh behind her hands.

"Who is this woman, anyway?" Giselle pointed toward Grace. "You're replacing me with that fat bitch?"

"Grace is a sweet, loving woman that I've come to care a great deal about," Toffer said. "I'm sorry, Giselle, if you didn't understand me the other day when I said we were done. But let me say it again. We're done. Please give me your keys and leave. Take the delivery boy home and fuck him. Maybe he'll give you the dinner for free."

Giselle's slap resounded through the room. Toffer ran his hand along his cheek and didn't move. The model stomped to her keys, fumbled with them until she'd freed two from her ring, which she promptly turned and threw at Grace.

"There, now you don't have to have copies made." Then she ran out the front door.

"Hey, man, somebody's gotta pay for this food and the fine chick didn't finish paying for it."

Toffer nodded and took out his wallet; he placed two hundred dollars in the man's outstretched hand.

"Thanks, Mr. Dawson. Later." Then he leaned toward Toffer. "Just between us dudes, I think you should have taken the skinny chick. She's freaking hot."

Millie broke out in apologies the minute the van pulled out of the driveway. Toffer held up his hand.

"This is my fault. I should have taken her keys earlier. It's been over for a long time; you know that."

Millie nodded, and then Rafe propelled his wife out the door.

"I'm sorry, Grace."

He was surprised when Grace laughed. "Toffer, I learned years ago not to pay attention to what women like that say about me. Besides, I knew that you wanted me."

"I want all of you."

"It would be a shame to waste that beautiful dinner. You did pay for it."

Toffer laughed. "Send it upstairs on the dumbwaiter. We'll use it for a little lesson in submission."

* * *

"Open." Grace sat up, fighting for her balance with her arms clipped behind her back, and took the offered bite of food into her mouth. She was naked, as she always was in the bedroom and she felt very vulnerable.

She watched Master take a bite of the steak and chew.

"Submission isn't just about sex. It's about giving up control. It's about compassion and building up trust. Learning to eat from my hand will build trust. I've been lax since you got here. You haven't stood in the corner once. Not in five days. And I've only whipped you once. Bite."

Grace took a bite of the potatoes. She'd been instructed not to talk until she was given permission. It was very hard to obey that instruction. She wanted to voice her opinion on the matter.

"I blame my laxness on the fact that I've been bewitched by you. The minute I saw you, I couldn't wait to fuck you. Tomorrow, we'll spend time in the dungeon. I'm going to teach you about delaying orgasm. And I'm going to teach you about how pain can turn into pleasure, which means I'm going to introduce you to the clit clamp."

Grace widened her eyes and took another bite. She'd been dreading that clit clamp. But his other words affected her more than the idea of the clamp. She bewitched him? Those words buried themselves in her brain and took root. He'd kicked a beautiful model out of his house and Grace bewitched him. Did she dare hope that he loved her? She knew that she was feeling love for him.

"Here's how tonight's going to work. When I'm done feeding you you're going to stand in the corner for thirty minutes. Then we'll watch some TV and go to bed, just like an old married couple. Except for the fact that I'm going to tie you to the bed before you go to sleep. You'll sleep bound to the bed frame."

Grace shook her head violently. There was no way she could sleep while she was tied up. No way at all.

"Yes. I'm impressed that you didn't talk, but that doesn't change what's going to happen. This will put you in a very submissive frame of mind for tomorrow. This involves trust, Lolly. You have to trust me not to bind you too tightly, not to make it so you would get hurt. Do you trust me, Grace?"

"Yes, Master."

"Good. Then let us begin."

Chapter Eleven

Note to self: Giving up control can be a magical thing.

To Do List:
Follow Master's instructions

Grace woke and tried to stretch. When her arms refused to budge she took a deep breath and told herself not to panic. Master was not in bed with her, but she knew that he was in the house somewhere. Maybe he was in the dungeon, getting ready for their "play date" as he'd called it last night.

The cuffs were locked together. A rope ran through them that was looped through a bar attached to Grace's nightstand. The leg cuffs were tied together with a rope and attached to the bed frame. Grace had fought terror last night when Toffer had tied her. She'd begged and pleaded with him not to do it. He'd stroked her hair and asked calmly if she wanted to use her safe word. She'd refused. When she was fully bound to the bed, he'd laid down next to her and jacked himself off while she watched. Then he'd cleaned up, turned out the light and gone to sleep.

He'd left enough leeway in the ropes that Grace could turn if she needed to, which she did, but still sleep didn't come. She lay awake for an hour listening to him snore softly. She fought panic several times, and finally fallen asleep with her face facing toward him.

Now she pulled on the ropes and found that they wouldn't budge. He must have tightened them up when he woke.

"Master?" The need to pee was growing. "Master, please? Where are you?"

"I'm here, Lolly." He came down the stairs from the dungeon, a smile on his face. "Sleep well?"

"Not really."

"That's too bad, because I liked it. We'll have to do this again. I know a man who attached his submissive's collar to the bed every night before they went to sleep. He said it was highly erotic and now I know what he meant."

"Master, I need to pee." Grace wiggled to make her point.

He laughed. "I'm sure you do." He undid the ropes quickly and patted her butt when she scooted past him. "Come to the dungeon door and knock when you're done, but don't come in."

Grace did her business, brushed her teeth and washed her face.

She stuck her tongue at the ropes as she walked by the bed. She may not have liked it, but she knew he did, and that made it a little better for her. She knocked on the door of the dungeon, her heart in her throat. Today was the day. She would get to see the dungeon and experience its thrills, and chills, firsthand.

Master opened the door and stepped onto the landing, closing the door behind him. "Leave Grace at the door. In here, you're Lolly, understand?"

"Yes, Master."

"Good. I'm sure you've noticed that I haven't put a collar on you. When you collar a sub it's very private and beautiful. It denotes that you're pledged to each other, she to submitting to you; you to taking care of her. I'm going to put a collar on you just for today, to put you in the right frame of mind. One of these days I might collar you permanently, but we have to discuss that, and its implications, before it happens."

Grace smiled. Butterflies were doing cartwheels in her belly.

"Kneel."

Grace knelt, her heart pounding as a slim leather collar went around her neck. Master fastened it at the front and slipped a small lock through the fastener. When he clicked the lock into place, she moaned.

"Let's go inside, Lolly."

He opened the door and led her inside. Grace stared at the room. Three walls and the ceiling were done totally in mirrors. In the center was a St. Andrew's Cross. It was lying flat, up enough off the ground so that the person who was bound to it could be easily accessible for sex. The odd wall contained an assortment of floggers, crops, and leather belts.

Set into the wall was a restraining bolt where a person could be tied.

A person? Who was she kidding? That person would be her. Against another wall sat a chair with restraints, and a refrigerator. A refrigerator? Grace raised her eyebrows and Master laughed.

"You never know what's going to come in handy. Go to the cross and lie down on it."

Grace fought to control her breath as Master strapped her to the cross. There were bindings on her ankles and thighs, on her wrists and upper arms, and around her waist. He walked around her, trailing his fingers along her skin.

When he was done, he gathered first one breast, and then the other in his hands. "I haven't paid enough attention to your breasts. They're wonderful, you know, and I've basically ignored them. Let's remedy my oversight, shall we?"

He took a nipple between each thumb and forefinger. He rolled it back and forth, pinching in various degrees while Grace worked to hold back moans. It felt so wonderful.

"Nice, plump nipples. Did you practice with your clamps?"

Master pulled her nipples upwards, lifting her breasts high in the air. Grace fought the urge to hiss her delight, and whispered, "Yes, Master."

"Good. I think I need a little taste."

He sucked first one nipple, and then the other. Then he pushed them together and sucked them both into his mouth. Grace moaned as he gathered both her nipples in his teeth and flicked his tongue over the nubs.

"Master."

He lifted up long enough to tell her to shush. Then his tongue went back to work on each nipple, laving each one with his tongue before taking it between his teeth and lightly biting them and nibbling around the aureole.

"You know what I think we need to buy? Little suction cups. I'd love to attach them and watch the pressure, and pleasure, spread throughout your body. Watch your nipples tighten inside them. They're such beautiful little nubs."

Grace was in heaven. Her nipples loved every minute of the attention. When the first nipple clamp was applied, her loud "ouch," filled the room.

"Silence, Lolly. If I need to gag you, I will. No more sounds."

The second clamp went on and Lolly bit her lip. The pain wasn't bad, and she'd felt the clamps before. Her mind knew that the real pain was just around the corner. The clit clamp couldn't be far behind the nipple clamps.

Master straddled her and pushed her breasts together, sliding his cock between them and pumping her.

"Do you like this, Lolly?"

"Yes, Master."

"Good. I do, too. But I have a few things I want to add, first."

When he got up Grace felt abandoned. She wanted him back, wanted the feel of his weight on her, the touch of his body.

"Lift your head." He slid a black blindfold over her eyes and Grace let out a cry.

"No, please, Master, I want to watch."

"Speak again without permission and I'll gag you."

She could hear him moving about, the opening and closing of the refrigerator door. What was he doing? Was he going to use whipped cream? That would be cool. She felt his presence between her outstretched legs. His fingers gently parted her nether lips. And then he waited. And waited. It seemed like hours, but Grace knew it had only been minutes.

The tip of something extremely cold touched her clit and Grace lifted off the table, biting off the second half of the word, "cold" before the object made its way down her slit and into her pussy.

It was cold, very, very, very cold.

"It's a glass cock," Master said. "I bought several just for you, in various shapes and designs. The site said they hold temperature very well, and can cause wonderful sensations. Tell me what you're feeling now."

"Cold. Very, very cold. Too cold."

"Oh, I don't think so. Your clit likes it." He pulled on her hardened nub and Grace moaned. Then she let out a scream as a clamp came down on her tender flesh.

"Master. No, please, no!"

He began to fuck her harder with the cock, the cold mixing with the now cooling temperature of her skin, melding together with the hotness coming from her clamped clit.

"I'm going to come. Master, I'm going to come!"

"Don't you dare. You do and you'll get twenty strokes from the crop. You'll come when I say."

Master pulled on the clamp and Grace tried to lift her bound body into it. She bit her lip and forced down the need to explode. It felt so fucking good.

"Please!" The moan reverberated through the room.

He pulled the glass cock from her and undid the clamps. Blood rushed back into her clit and nipples.

"No. You can wait."

The urge to come was maddening. She was right on the edge, afraid that the slightest bit of sensation would drive her over.

He crouched next to her ear. "Was the pain good? Did you like it?"

"Yes, Master."

"When you come it will be like nothing you've ever felt before. It won't be totally from the pain. It will be a mixture of that, and of delaying your gratification. You have to trust me to guide you through this."

The clamps were reapplied to her nipples. This time there was a little less pressure than last time. She didn't jump when he clamped her clit this time. She heard him attach the chains together and then felt a pull on the clamps as he attached it to a chain that was above her. The glass cock was slipped back inside her.

"Three minutes, Lolly. How much the chains are pulled depends on you. If you move, you will pull on the clamps and increase your sensations. If I were you, I would hold still. You have three minutes."

He moved away from her and Grace tried to sense where he was. She knew he was watching her. She moved and the chains on her clamps, attached to the one in the ceiling, tightened and pulled.

"Ouch, Master, please."

"Two and a half more minutes. Close your eyes and concentrate. Concentrate on what you're feeling."

Close her eyes? She was already blindfolded. She did as he said, and a whole new sensation came over her. She could almost see him watching her. That thought pushed her even farther and she wiggled, pulling on the chain and increasing her sensations.

"Master! I can't help it. I've got to come."

"Don't do it, Lolly. Your punishment may well be missing out on my other plans for the afternoon."

Grace relaxed, trying to control her breathing. She counted in her brain to take her mind off the feelings building inside her body. In the back of her mind, she heard Master say there was forty-five more seconds.

Don't come. Don't come. Don't come.

"Good girl. I'm so proud of you. You look so beautiful. Twenty more seconds."

Don't come. Don't come. Don't come.

The tension on her clips was released, and the clamps came off quickly.

"Very good, my Lolly-girl. All done."

"May I come now, Master?" Her breathing was ragged. Master pulled the blindfold from her eyes as he straddled her.

"Not yet." He gathered her breasts, poured warm oil between them and slid himself inside the cavern they made.

"So good. Is the cock still cold?"

"Yes, Sir."

"Good. When I come, then you can come, not before. Make sure the cock stays in your pussy."

Each thrust of his cock between her breasts brought Grace a step closer to orgasm. She knew that when she came it would be hot, blowing the roof off anything she'd ever felt. Master reached down and pinched her nipples, never stopping his thrusts.

"Who owns these nipples?"

"You do, Master."

I can't hold on, please!

"And that glass-filled pussy?"

"You do, Master. Please, I can't wait, please!"

"Then say it again!"

"You own my pussy. You do. Master, Master, I belong to you!"

Grace felt the first streams of his come hit her chin.

"Grace, fuck, need, love, oh…"

He increased the pressure on her breasts and she knew she'd be sore in the morning, but she didn't care, she'd be sore in all the places for what she just heard him say. He loved her, he really did.

She knew she could come now and she wiggled to try and get the cock inside her to come into contact with her clit. She lifted her head when Master turned and buried his face between her thighs. His teeth found her clit and she came, screaming out her pleasure as he ran his tongue back and forth between her captured flesh.

When her orgasm subsided he ran his tongue up and down her pussy, pulling the cock from it gently and replacing it with his tongue. He licked her folds over and over, and then stood and waggled the cock at her.

"It's still cold," he said with wonder in his voice.

"Not near as cold as it was," Grace said.

"Did you enjoy that, Lolly-girl?"

"Yes, Master."

He undid the bindings and helped her to her feet. She was unsteady and he pulled her into his arms.

"I think it's time for a rest."

He led them to the bed and when they were nestled between the covers he fell asleep immediately. Grace's flesh was still throbbing. She rose up on an elbow and stared at him. It was amazing to her that since their first fight, she'd never once thought of him as Drake Dawson. To her, he was Toffer Shelley. She fit easily into Toffer's world. Where, she wondered, would she fit into Drake's?

* * *

Giselle sat in her car, just down the road from Drake's house. That fucking bastard! How dare he throw her over for a fat bitch? So she had big tits, so what? Any doctor in L.A. could give her big jugs, too.

She imagined him up there, fucking her in the bed they'd once made love in. Drake had never wanted a commitment, she knew that. And she ignored the fact that more than a year ago he'd told her that he thought they should break things off.

She'd always managed to pull him back in when he needed someone beautiful on his arm at a premiere, or at an awards event. What would the paparazzi think if he showed up with little Miss Tubby? He'd be a laughing stock in looks-conscious Hollywood.

She slunk down in her seat as Drake's Porsche sped by. He and the bitch were in the front seat, laughing and talking. She waited a few beats and then fell in behind them. It wasn't hard to tail them unseen in the Los Angeles traffic. When he parked at the zoo and got out, baseball cap pulled down low to hide his face, Giselle laughed.

She pulled out her phone and punched in a number.

"Where's your camera?"

"Baby, you know I don't go anywhere without my camera. Got it right here."

"How soon can you get to the zoo?"

"For?"

"For an exclusive picture of Drake Dawson and his girlfriend for next Monday's edition of your little rag."

"Sweetie, from what I hear, the two of you are old news. It's all over town that he kicked you out of his house for some chick the other day."

Giselle fumed. Prick of a delivery boy!

"Not me, moron. The fat chick he's fucking."

The line went quiet.

"You call anyone else?"

"If you're not here in ten minutes, I will."

"I'll be there ASAP. Don't sell me out, baby, and I'll help you with your payback."

"Just get your ass over here."

Chapter Twelve

Note to self: Dreams can come true, in more ways than one!

To Do List:
Print out contract, sign and mail it in
Call parents, call Lindsey, call Becca and tell them good news
Prepare great dinner for Toffer

The dining room was all set. Lit candles lined the available surfaces. One place had been set at the table for Master; a large pillow was next to his chair for her to kneel on. She wanted tonight to be perfect. It was Wednesday, which meant there was only a few more days left of their peaceful existence together.

Despite their fun time at the zoo on Sunday, and the wonderful sex they'd shared that night, Toffer had never once mentioned making anything permanent, and Grace wasn't counting her chickens.

Preston had called earlier in the day to say that, while the hearing was still on, it was going to be a slam-dunk in her favor. He said he had a surprise witness who would refute the story being told, but he wouldn't tell her who it was.

And then, of course, there was her story. The online publisher that she'd sent several items to had e-mailed her to say they were interested in publishing it in an anthology. He said they were considering two more, and wanted to know when Grace would be finished with her novel. Remembering the conversation made her feel as if she was walking on the moon.

Grace listened at the front door for the sound of the gate. When it was activated she rushed inside to the dining room, quickly lit the smaller candles on the table, discarded her clothing and bent over the dining room table. She spread her legs wide and laid her head on the table.

Toffer's low whistle from the doorway told her that he liked what he saw.

"Yummy. That's quite an appetizer you've laid out, Lolly."

"Thank you, Master." She shivered as he caressed her behind.

"What's for dinner?"

"Millie cooked lasagna. She said it was your favorite."

"Yummy again. What's the occasion? Besides the fact that my beautiful submissive is draped over my dining room table, ready to be fucked?"

"I sold a story."

Toffer pulled her back into him, twirling her around and around as he planted kisses on her neck.

"Baby, that's fantastic! To who?"

She explained the details as Toffer sat down and turned her toward him. When she was done he kissed her, his tongue taking possession of her mouth until she groaned.

"This calls for a celebration." His voice was low as he rained kisses around her mouth. "But first, dinner, because I'm starved."

* * *

The chair was chilly against Grace's bare behind. She sat straight, her legs spread, feeling very vulnerable, and very excited. She pulled against the ropes that held her arms to the chair, held her legs open and tied to the legs.

"Bite." Master held out a forkful of lasagna, then helped himself to one while she chewed.

"Millie's outdone herself. This is really, really good. And the wine is very sweet."

"Yes, Master."

He took a sip of wine, and then took another one and leaned in close to Grace. When he kissed her, he transferred some of the liquid to her mouth.

"Your mouth makes it all the more sweet." His voice was tender. He trailed his fingers up and down her naked thighs, lightly running the tips over her mons.

"You don't like sitting naked at the table, I can tell. Sometimes it's good to try things outside your comfort zone. Tell me what you're feeling right now."

"Strange. This is really the first time I've been naked in this part of the house, and to sit here and be fed while you are clothed, well, it makes me feel very exposed."

"Good. That's how I like my Lolly-girl, exposed to me." He pushed aside her pussy lips and dipped his fingers into her wetness. "So very ready for me."

He murmured his approval as she licked her juices from his offered fingers.

When the plate was empty, Master pushed it back. "How shall we celebrate? Shall we take our dessert up to the hot tub? What's for dessert, anyway?"

"Cheesecake."

"Yum, another one of my favorites. Send a few slices, the wine and some utensils up in the dumbwaiter. I'm going upstairs. Meet me at the hot tub in five minutes."

He quickly untied her, kissed her and left the room.

Grace quickly performed her chores, sending the requested items upstairs. She found Master already ensconced in the tub. She sat the tray on the nearby table.

"Can I feed you this time?" Grace climbed into the water and straddled Master's lap. He was already hard, his cock rubbing against her thigh. She offered him a bite of cheesecake and he took it with a smile.

"Tell me what selling a story means to you, not mentally, but to your situation in life. How does this change things for you?"

Grace's heart was beating fast. What was he asking? Could it be possible that he wanted her to stay? She'd dreamt about it, wanted it to happen. But he'd never mentioned it.

"Well, it's not like I'm getting a million dollar advance or anything. It's just a short story. I'm hoping it will lead to bigger things."

"Hum. Feed me some more. I think I like this role reversal." Toffer stretched out his arms on the back of the tub and Grace continued to give him the treat, taking occasional bites to satisfy her sweet tooth.

When Master dipped his fingers into the cake and raised his eyebrows up and down, Grace smiled. When he coated both nipples with cheesecake, she shivered. He coated the aureole and then leaned back.

"Eat your dessert, Lolly. Earn your nickname, again."

Their eyes locked as Grace raised a breast, trailing her tongue through the creamy dessert. The sugary cake tasted wonderful against the saltiness of her skin. More than the taste, however, was the total look of fascination that had come over her Master's face.

"Is this what you wanted, Master?" She snaked her tongue to her nipple, taking it into her mouth and sucking. The groan that escaped his mouth let her know that was exactly what he wanted. She cleaned one breast of the cake, and then turned to the other.

When she reached the nipple, Toffer's tongue mingled with hers as they licked the treat off together. When the food was gone he ran his arms up her spine. "You know what I'm going to do to you tonight, sweet Gracie?"

Grace shook her head and he pulled her in for a kiss. When their lips parted he held her face close to his.

"I'm going to fuck your sweet ass. I was going to wait until Saturday, until after the party, but I decided that I just couldn't wait that long. It's been hell waiting this long."

He kissed her again and then dropped his head down to lavish attention on her nipples. He pushed them together and took them both in his mouth at the same time, biting gently, and then biting harder until Grace let out a harsh moan of need.

Toffer massaged her breasts as he lifted his face back to hers. "You ready for me to fuck your ass, Lolly? Tell me."

"Yes, Master. I want it." The world was spinning. This was something she'd wanted to do for a long time. Part way through the week she'd wondered why he hadn't brought it up. Now she knew that he was waiting for just the right time.

He pushed her into a standing position, and then reached over the side of the tub to retrieve a condom and a bottle of lube. Grace sighed and he smiled.

"I want you to enjoy this, Lolly. I'm not going to lie to you. Initially, it might hurt, but if it does, you tell me and I'll slow down. You have permission to speak whenever you want."

Grace nodded and smiled at him.

"Kneel right here, with your legs spread." He guided her into a kneeling position on one of the built-in seats. She could feel the jet from the machine pushing the water into her thigh.

"Put your clitty into the jet stream."

Grace bent a little more and her clit came into contact with the pulsating water. It felt like a million tiny fingers were dancing over her clit.

"Oh, oh, Master, I'm gonna come."

"Better not. Keep your clitty moving in the stream, I want it to stimulate you, but I don't want you to come without my permission. Do you understand, Grace? You know the rule and if you come before I say, you'll sleep tied to the bed as punishment, and I know how you hate that."

Grace nodded as she wiggled in the water. The sensation was overwhelming and it couldn't get any better, or so she thought. Moments later she gripped the sides of the tub harder as Toffer's slicked up fingers began to probe her rosette. He applied subtle pressure, backed off, and then applied it again.

"So very sweet," he said softly in her ear. "Lolly is all ready for her Master. She wants his cock in her ass, buried deep, taking her and making her fully his." As he pushed his fingers past her opening, Grace sighed. She'd been wearing the plugs regularly, so the invasion of his finger didn't hurt. She felt full and open as she bucked against the stream and pushed herself back onto his finger.

He added another one and twisted them gently in her behind. "So very beautiful."

Grace fought against the need to come. Her clit felt as if it was on fire each time so she moved it away from the hardest part of the stream. She could almost hear it screaming at her to "go back, go back."

Toffer moved his fingers back and forth and stroked her back with his free hand. When he took his fingers away, Grace thought she would die.

"Master, please, I need you. I want you. Please."

"Do you, Lolly?" He placed the tip of his cock at her opening and pushed, pulling back before he could break into her bud. He moved it back and forth several more times before positioning her back over the stream, and finally pushing his cock fully past her muscle into the soft muscles beyond.

A tingling sensation moved through her and Grace whimpered. Toffer stroked her back again and grabbed her hips. His cock filled her so much more than the plug that she thought she would die right on the spot. She wasn't sure she would be able to handle this. It was too much; he was too big.

"Do you want this?" He pushed in further and Grace tried to move away.

"Too big, too big. I can't, please..."

She moved again and her clit slid into full contact with the stream and she came, screaming out for more over and over before the words had even registered in her brain.

Toffer obliged her, pushing himself inside her slowly as he centered her clit over the jet. Grace came again, whimpering as overwhelming bliss spread through her.

"Master, oh Master, so good. So very good."

"Do you like it, baby?"

"Yes, Toffer, oh god, yes!"

When he was totally inside her he laid his head on her shoulder. "You're mine, Gracie, all mine."

Grace sighed and moved her lips toward his. "I'm yours, all yours."

When their lips were locked together, he began to rock into her, gently at first and then increasing his thrusts as she moaned her desire. His increased thrusts put her back into contact with the stream. Grace tried to move away and he slapped her ass, ordering her back into the jet.

"Can't, too much."

"You can. One more time on my command, especially since you came twice on your own, earning a punishment."

Grace heard the humor in his voice. His breathing was labored and she knew that he wouldn't last long. The water massaged her aching clit and she moved away from it, waiting for her Master's command. It was hard though, to stay away. Even though her clit was aching from overuse, it still wanted attention, still was demanding to be brought to completion again.

"Are you ready?" Toffer sounded as if he'd just finished running a marathon and Grace couldn't help but smile.

"Yes, Master."

"Then come with me, Lolly. Come now!"

He slapped himself into her with such force that she thought they might tumble out of the tub. And then they both came, their frenzied movements sending sprays of water over the edge of the hot tub and out onto the deck. When the tremors had subsided, Toffer ordered Grace to stay in the tub. He went inside to dispose of the condom and then pulled Grace into his arms, pressing her back against his chest as he settled back into the tub.

"You realize you called me, Toffer, don't you?"

Grace bit her lip. "I'm sorry, Master."

"That's all right. I think it just means you like sleeping tied up next to me, cause you earned another night of punishment."

He kissed her temple. "I want to ask you something, Grace. If you didn't have your job to go back to, would you stay here?"

"In California?" Her heart beat faster.

"In my house. With me."

She turned to look into his eyes. "Truly?"

"Yes. Don't answer now. Just think about it."

"What exactly am I supposed to think about? Being your submissive?"

"It's not exactly romantic to propose in a hot tub after you've just fucked a woman silly, but I think having you as my submissive, and my wife, would be an awesome thing."

"Toffer, we live in totally different worlds."

"It doesn't matter. Like I told you the first night here, my being Drake Dawson doesn't change anything between us. I love you, Grace. I've loved you for days now. Don't answer just yet. But please don't rule it out, either."

Grace bit her lip and he laughed.

"You keep biting your lip and there won't be anything left of it."

"I love you, too. But I was married once before and it was a disaster."

"Yes, but your husband wasn't me. Think about it. You can give me your answer before you leave on Monday."

Monday. Grace shook her head. "The day before Valentine's Day. The day before my hearing."

"From what you said, Preston thinks it's a slam dunk. You have no reason to lose your job because of these stupid accusations. But if you wanted to quit and move out here at the end of the year that would be a different story altogether."

He pulled her close to him and kissed her softly. "We could be together. It doesn't matter what other people think, or that we live in two different worlds. Here we live in our world. The world of Toffer and Lolly. No one has to know about that world except the two of us. And we would be very, very, very happy."

Grace didn't answer. This was what she had been thinking of for weeks. She and Toffer had formed a bond several days after getting to know one another. But the truth of the matter was that when he was Toffer, things had been great. When he was Drake Dawson, she had been scared. She'd forced herself to face those fears, but in the long run would they really be able to stay in their own world, cocooned together against the world?

"I'll think about it."

"Promise."

"I promise, Master."

"Then let's go to bed before we end up looking like prunes. Besides, I have a sub to tie-up for the evening." He grinned and swatted her behind as she scurried toward the bathroom to dry off.

Chapter Thirteen

Note to self: Success can come into your life both personally and professionally if you let it. Don't sabotage yourself. Think about your answer to Toffer's question carefully.

To Do List:
Wrap Lindsey's birthday present
Iron dress for party
Call Preston about Tuesday's hearing

As the hearing date grew closer and closer, Grace got more and more nervous. Despite Toffer's reassurances she was sure that something would happen at the last minute to cause her world to come tumbling down.

But would that be a bad thing? She had Toffer now, she belonged to him. When he'd untied her on Thursday morning she'd asked if he'd been serious about marriage, or if it had been the wine talking. For an answer, he'd kissed her so deeply she thought his tongue would merge with her own. Then he'd left without another word.

The next two days had been wonderful. They'd talked and played as if they were an old married couple. So if the hearing went south, would it be a bad thing? Grace shook her head. She didn't want to have her reputation as a teacher tarnished by false accusations. But if she lived with Toffer, would it matter? And would the tabloids get hold of the information and banter her name around as the "blackmailing wife of Drake Dawson?"

She shook her head. The party was tonight. Peter had a full day planned with Lindsey that included a day out at the movies, one of Lindsey's favorite activities. Then the couple would have dinner while everyone invaded their home. The party planner had assured Grace on Friday that they had "the decorating specs" down to a science and it would only take them a few hours to prepare.

Grace and Toffer were scheduled to meet the organizers at 7:15, moments after Peter and Lindsey left. Now she sat in front of her laptop, trying to finish the last chapter of her mystery novel and not think about Toffer, not think about what he'd proposed.

But how could she not? Everything depended on her answer. She loved him. There was no doubt about that. But she was almost forty years old, and thinking about taking a huge step away from her comfort zone.

The idea was horribly frightening, and wonderfully exciting. She imagined herself working out of the home she was sitting in, enjoying lunches with Millie and putting her collar on every day when the woman and her husband left.

Her collar. That idea of a collar represented so much. Toffer had put one on her for their sessions in the dungeon. He'd told her last night that if she accepted his proposal they'd have an official collaring ceremony after the party, and that he would expect her to wear the collar when they were alone in the house together. If there were people about he had a short silver chain, holding a charm with the letter "T" that she would wear around her neck.

She closed her eyes and imagined her life. Would he make her sleep tied to the bed every night? He had the last three nights. Of course, he'd say that had been for punishment from the hot tub session on Wednesday night. The memory of that night brought a huge smile to Grace's face. Despite the original discomfort of taking him that way she'd loved every minute of it. She'd loved everything they'd done together.

Would she love it if it had been someone other than Toffer as her Master? She tightened her eyes and tried to think of her ex in that position. She shuddered in disgust. Likewise, none of the men she'd "dated" since her divorce fit well into her image of a loving dominant that would take care of her…that she could serve and be totally submissive to.

She closed her laptop and went in search of Toffer. She found him in the workout room, building up those beautiful muscles that women swooned over.

"Done already?" He huffed out as he curled his arms up and down.

"Not yet. I just wanted to tell you that I've made my decision."

He set the weights down and crossed to her.

"And?"

"The answer is yes; I'll marry you." She pressed her lips to his in a gentle kiss and he enveloped her in a bear hug.

"I love you. I'll always love you. You won't regret this. I promise."

"I know. I love you, too."

He pulled back and laughed. "I've got you all sweaty. Let's go up and shower together before the party."

"Anything you say, Master."

"No. Right now I want us to make love as Christopher Shelley and Grace Kinison. Because Christopher is who you're marrying. He'll be your Master, yes, but right now he's going to be your lover."

Grace melted into his chest. "Then take me upstairs and ravish me. Make good on your promise to always love me."

Toffer raised his eyebrows and gave her a cocky grin.

"After you, sweet one."

When they were in the bathroom they undressed each other, laughing as they pulled clothing from each other's bodies. The shower was huge, an eight by eight square with multiple showerheads on three walls. Toffer turned them all on and pulled the removable showerhead from one of its moorings.

He turned it to pulse and pulled Grace back against his body, running the water over her breasts and pussy until she cried out.

"All rules are suspended for now, Grace. I want you to come, and come, and come. I want to hear you, feel you, smell your sweet juices, taste you."

Toffer dropped the showerhead and turned her. He moved her until her back was against the wall, then he dropped to his knees.

"Spread your legs." Grace put her hands on either side of her hips and spread her legs as far as they would go. She moaned when Toffer parted her lips and ran his tongue up and down her slick folds.

"So very good," he whispered. His breath tickled her clit and she giggled. Seconds later, the giggle turned into a scream as he sucked the bud into her mouth and Grace came. She ground herself against his face as he licked and nibbled.

"Again." His words were muffled as he continued his assault. Grace closed her eyes and allowed the sheer bliss of his tongue to spread through her body. He lapped at her clit, sending shivers down her spine as his tongue moved down her folds and pushed inside her wetness.

"Toffer! I need you inside me. Now!"

"But I am inside you. I'm inside your sweet little pussy."

"No, I want your cock!"

"Don't you like my tongue?" He teased her by darting his tongue in and out of her, holding her close by clasping her ass in his hands and pushing her into his face.

"You're killing me!" He ignored her words and continued to lick. His talented tongue sent her over the edge again and she begged him to fuck her.

Toffer lay down on the slick floor. He moved his head out of the water stream and held out his arms.

"Come here, baby."

Grace knelt over him. She held herself over his erection.

"Is it my turn to tease you?"

Toffer grinned, grabbed her hips and brought her down onto his cock. She gasped and laughed.

"Spoil sport. Of course, I can always tease you with these." She pushed her breasts together, pulling on her nipples as she rocked back and forth on his cock. The look of hunger on Toffer's face was priceless.

"Mine," he growled. "Lean down."

"No."

He slapped her ass, the sting accentuated by the water slapping against her backside.

"Lean down. Give me that nipple, now."

"Never." She worked to keep from laughing.

He slapped her ass again, and then flipped her onto her side, his cock still inside her as he lowered his head and captured a nipple. She cradled his head against her breast. His thrusts increased as he sucked her nipple.

When he pushed her onto her back and rose above her, she marveled at the look of pleasure that lit his face. He thrust gently back and forth, and then said, "You're mine, Grace. Forever."

"Forever." Their words echoed in the shower, and then he came, their gazes locking as he gently rocked back and forth.

When he'd collapsed on top of her, she whispered, "No protection."

"I don't care," he answered. "I hope we made a baby. Part of you, and part of me. The best of both of us."

Her heart swelled at his words. She had found the perfect man in Christopher Shelley. And she never planned to let him go.

Toffer stood and helped Grace up.

"Now that we've used up all the hot water, shall we bathe in the cold shower?"

"Can we stay here forever? I don't want to share you with anyone else tonight."

"What about Lindsey's party?" He nibbled on her lips, then grabbed the soap and lathered up her breasts.

"I know." Grace really looked forward to seeing Lindsey. But with her body tingling from Toffer's lovemaking, she couldn't help but want to stay in his arms.

"We'll continue this later, Lolly." He grinned and kissed her again.

"As you wish, Master."

* * *

Even though she'd greeted Lindsey at the door, Grace didn't get a chance to really talk to her until more than two hours into the party. People had surrounded Lindsey to wish her well, and even though she'd tried to latch onto Grace, she'd been lost in the crowd.

When Grace heard her friend's voice whisper in her ear several hours later, she'd laughed.

"Get upstairs, now! I want to talk to you."

Lindsey had slammed the door of the office once they were upstairs.

"You bitch! How could you?"

"Peter wanted it to be a surprise," Grace said innocently, knowing full well that not telling her about the party wasn't what Lindsey meant.

"I'm talking about Toffer. You've been staying with him for more than a week and you didn't call me? You didn't tell me that you and he were having sex? Geeze, my best friend develops a relationship with the most eligible bachelor in Hollywood and I have to find out about it at least a week after it's happened. You owe me some gossip, woman! So spill. Now!"

Grace laughed as the women embraced. She had been determined not to tell Lindsey that she and Toffer were engaged. She didn't want to ruin the party that was supposed to be for her friend. Now she knew that if she waited to tell her, Lindsey would never forgive her.

"Can you keep a secret?"

"Depends." Lindsey put her hands on her hips and cocked her head.

"He asked me to marry him, and I said yes."

The look of total shock on Lindsey's face made Grace giggle.

"You'll live here! We can see each other all the time! Maybe you can write for the show! Oh my stars! I can't wait to tell Peter."

Lindsey ran for the door and Grace pulled her back. "Not now! This is your moment and Peter has gone to a lot of trouble. I don't want to overpower it with this. Besides I don't want to make everything known until Toffer and I have talked through the details. I just told him yes this afternoon."

"So is he good in bed? No, wait, don't answer that. I don't want to ruin the fantasy."

Grace raised her eyebrows and Lindsey laughed.

"Hey, I'm only human!" They headed downstairs arm in arm, weaving through the crowd toward the kitchen. Toffer was talking to someone that Grace didn't know. She heard people refer to him as Drake several times and she laughed. It was still difficult to think of him as Drake Dawson. To her that would be a work persona, just like her nom de plume would be her work persona.

Peter pulled her in for a brotherly hug and then kissed her cheek. "Can I be the first to say 'Hello, Mrs. Shelley?'"

Grace blushed and Lindsey did a dance of happiness.

"Hey, count me in on this," Toffer said, joining the group and pulling Grace into a backward embrace.

He started to open his mouth again when a saccharine voice sounded from the doorway.

"Well, isn't that sweet. They're recreating the pose that made the front page of the paper."

Giselle stepped into the room and threw a handful of papers on the counter.

"What are you doing here?" Toffer's voice was icy. "I don't believe you're on the guest list."

"What's one more friend at a party," Giselle said. "Besides, I wanted to be the first to congratulate you on your Valentine's present."

"My what?"

She held up a tabloid newspaper and grinned evilly. On the front cover was a large photo of Grace and Toffer at the zoo. Grace's back was pressed to Toffer's front, one of his hands lightly cupping a breast. Their lips were locked in a heated kiss. The headline read "A HUGE VALENTINE FOR DRAKE."

Giselle took a paper off the stack that she'd laid on the counter. "Here, let me read it for you."

"Seems Drake Dawson's tastes are changing, which is good news for all the large ladies in the land. The oh so handsome actor, who usually can be seen sporting models around town, was spotted at the Los Angeles Zoo on Sunday with a buxom brunette on his arm who seemed to be more than just a friend. Onlookers may not have recognized the gorgeous ladies' man hidden behind the wall of his new paramour, but that was him, acting like a tourist and a lovesick schoolboy."

Grace felt her stomach drop to the floor. *The wall of his new paramour? They mean me. I'm the wall. I'm the HUGE Valentine present.*

"Toffer?"

"You bitch. This woman wouldn't, she couldn't...fuck." His words were strangled and Grace turned to see the redness of his face. Was he mad, or embarrassed that they'd been caught? That everyone had seen him kissing her in public? He'd asked her to marry him. Would he hide her away in the hills to keep from being seen with her?

"Grace, I'm so sorry..."

"Yes, Grace, he's sorry that you were found out. I mean, obviously that's why he wore that ridiculous hat, so that no one would notice him with you, I mean he never wore it when he was out with me. You're bad for his image and he knows it. And she couldn't what, *Toffer*, replace me? Well, we all know that."

Grace backed away from Toffer, their gazes locked.

"Get out," he said, and then reached for Grace.

She turned and bolted through the crowd, pushing past elbows and shoulders of people who had gathered to watch the drama.

"Not you! Grace! Get back here." Toffer's voice rang out, but Grace kept pushing through the group to the stairs. She ran upstairs to find her purse, which she'd stored in Lindsey's closet. She could hear Lindsey yelling for the "fucking bitch to get the hell out of my house."

Grace grabbed her purse, opened it to make sure she'd brought her wallet, and then bolted for the front door. Toffer's words rang in her ear. "This woman wouldn't, she couldn't…"

She ran out the door right into a couple who had just arrived in a taxi.

"Leaving already? I hope this party's not that bad." The woman laughed as Grace ducked inside the cab.

"Take me to the airport, please."

A dam of tears burst as the taxi rolled down the driveway.

"Lady, you OK?"

"Fine. Please, just go."

Her tears fell as Toffer's words played over and over in her brain, "She wouldn't, she couldn't. Get out. Get out. Get out."

Was it her imagination or had he turned to look at Giselle after he'd said those words? Grace shook her head. No, he'd been looking at her. How could he have fooled her so? And why did he do it? Did he get kicks off deflating a woman's ego? He'd asked her to marry him, and she'd fallen for it. She'd told him yes. When was he going to tell her the truth…that she didn't fit into his world.

Now he didn't have to. The newspaper and his paper-thin girlfriend had done it for him. Damn them all to hell.

At the airport, she paid the taxi driver and went inside to check the schedule. The next plane for Denver didn't leave for another three hours. That was too long to wait. She wanted out of California, now. And she didn't care if she ever came back.

Grace went into the bathroom to get her breathing under control. She washed her splotchy face and walked into the main terminal. She rented a car and asked for directions out of the city. A check of her watch showed her that it was just after ten. If she drove for eight hours she would make it to Las Vegas and get a room there.

Her cell phone rang as she merged onto the 105 East. She ignored it and seconds after the ringing stopped it started again. At the fourth call, as Grace was merging onto the 605 North, she turned the phone off and fought back tears.

Life with Toffer was over. It had been magical to experience new things with him. She wondered again about his asking her to marry him, and then saying, "this woman couldn't…" without finishing the statement. What did he mean? She couldn't do what? Satisfy him? Make him happy? Be more than just a decent fuck?

If that was the truth, then why did he ask her to marry him, to move in with him? Why hadn't he turned to Giselle and shouted that no matter her size, he loved Grace and didn't want to live without her. His order to get out rang in her ear.

Still, a nagging in the back of her brain told her that he hadn't been talking to her. He'd been talking to Giselle. But he still hadn't stood up for her. She debated with the part of her that told her to turn around and go back to Lindsey's house. She was running away from a bad situation like an immature child.

She drove and drove as the situation played out in her brain. Then she stopped outside Barstow to get some very expensive gas. She checked her cell phone, and saw seventeen missed calls from Toffer's cell phone, nine from his house phone, three from her parents and ten from Lindsey's house. The mail envelope in the left-hand corner of the screen blinked furiously.

She knew that she should go back and straighten things out. But confrontations weren't her strong point. She had a battle on Valentine's Day that was going to be a doozy.

Valentine's Day. She shook her head. It wasn't one of her favorite holidays, since she hadn't anyone to celebrate it with. Until this year.

This woman wouldn't, she couldn't... Grace shook her head. Had she learned nothing through the years except to run away from things? Maybe Toffer was going to say that she couldn't be replaced by anyone, that she wouldn't fall for Giselle's stupid tricks.

She closed her eyes and imagined Toffer as he yelled for her to get out. He had been looking at Grace, but when the words came out he'd turned to stare at Giselle. It wasn't Grace he was telling to leave, it was Giselle.

Grace retrieved her messages and listened as Toffer begged and pleaded with her to come back.

"Baby, please! Where are you? You know how much you mean to me. Don't let her win. Come back to me. Call me."

The next few messages were the same mettle, varying from Toffer to Lindsey to her mother, all begging for a call. And then one of them made her laugh. "Lolly, this is your Master. If you don't call this instant you will stand in the corner for the rest of your natural born life, and the time you're not in a corner, you'll be over my knee. Do you understand me? Call me immediately!"

She took a deep breath and dialed his cell.

"Where the hell are you?"

"In a rental car, heading for Las Vegas."

"I'll meet you at the Luxor. I'll fly, but I think you'll still get there before me. If I'm not there, get us a room. You've got quite a punishment coming, young lady."

The phone went dead and Grace stared at it.

She did? This was his fault, not hers. Or maybe it was a mixture of the two. She was the one who had run. But she'd run because he hadn't stood up for her. She stared the engine and pointed the car north.

Grace mentally kicked herself. She was allowing her past experiences with Jesse to cloud her judgment. She'd have to explain this to Toffer, and hope that he understood.

* * *

Grace fought the Las Vegas traffic, parked at the hotel and, finding that Toffer wasn't there yet, registered herself. Once upstairs, she called and left the room number on his voice mail. She took a shower and was just wrapping herself in a towel when a knock came on the door.

She looked through the peephole and smiled when she saw Toffer staring back at her. Grace opened the door and he stood still, staring at her. She stepped aside as he brushed through, slammed the door and pressed her into the wall for a harsh kiss.

"Don't you ever run from me again. Is that the way you handle fights? To run? Shit, Grace, you didn't give me a chance to say anything."

"You said, that I couldn't. And then you told me to get out."

"No, I told Giselle to get out. I was looking at you, true, but that's because I wanted everyone to see that I loved you, that I couldn't take my eyes off you. I was angry and couldn't find the right words to tell her that you would never pull a stunt like she'd pulled, that you were more of a woman than she ever was. That I loved you more than anything in the world."

"I'm so sorry. I just don't deal with confrontations very well."

"Why? Tell me why you ran so far. I expected to find you back at the house."

Grace looked away, and Toffer put his fingers on her chin to bring her face back in line with his.

"Why, baby?"

"My ex, Jesse? When we broke up, he did it publicly. The look on your face, and the words get out, they threw me back to a really bad place and I freaked. Please forgive me."

"Only if you forgive me. I'm so sorry. I love you and I would never do anything to hurt you. You have to believe that."

"I love you too, Toffer. I know you'd never hurt me, but I allowed old insecurities to come into play."

"I want us to get married, tonight." His voice held a note of finality and Grace stared at him, dumbfounded.

"Excuse me?"

"We're getting married. Right now. Lindsey and Peter are in their own room waiting to stand up for us. You want Elvis? Or you want more traditional?"

"Toffer, I…"

"Don't argue with me, Grace. I don't ever want to take the chance of losing you. This will bind us forever. So what's it gonna be?"

Grace threw her head back and laughed. "Well, since we're in Las Vegas…"

Chapter Fourteen

Note to self: Try not to stare at your ring finger too much. It gives away the fact that you are blissfully happy.

To Do List:
Change name on driver's license
Change name on bank accounts
Call moving companies about boxing up house
Attend hearing about employment

The boardroom at the high school was packed. Preston said it was because of the tabloid pictures of Grace and Drake Dawson kissing.

"Everyone wants to see the woman who captured Drake Dawson's heart," Preston said. "Especially since it was all over the news last night that the two of you tied the knot in Las Vegas."

Grace kissed her husband. *Her husband.* The idea still made her shake her head. They'd been wed at one of the numerous Elvis chapels in Las Vegas. And Toffer had surprised Grace by presenting her with his grandmother's wedding ring. It was a beautiful antique setting with an absolutely stunning diamond.

They'd bought a ring for him from the chapel, and she promised to replace it with something better at a later date.

"No way," he'd said. "This is my wedding ring and I love it, though not as much as I love my wife."

Lindsey and Peter had been ecstatic, and after the wedding, they'd hit a few casinos and had breakfast at a buffet on the strip.

"So romantic," Grace teased Toffer, who had laughed.

"So original," he'd countered. "Getting married in Las Vegas. Who woulda thought it?"

And the paparazzi had followed them everywhere, anxious to get photos of the newlyweds.

"They're quick," Grace had said.

"I called them before I left L.A. Then I had my agent call with the name of the chapel. I wanted to counter-act the crap that Giselle had them print. I wanted them to see our wedding, and see how much I love you. To see that no one could ever mean more to me than you."

Grace had cried, and he'd kissed away her tears as the cameras flashed.

Now she stared at the standing-room only crowd. Joe Watson was sitting stone-faced at the main table. Frank Medina had approached to shake their hands.

"This shouldn't take long. Dominic has already admitted that everything he said was false. He said he wanted you to hurt, just like he had when he'd failed Senior English."

"Did he say anything about Watson putting him up to it?" Toffer's voice was harsh.

"No, and unfortunately there is nothing we can prove without him telling us. Watson knows, however, that I know the truth. I've told him that he needs to find another job before I find a reason to fire him."

"Grace, I have to ask you something. It's obvious that Watson has been harassing you, trying to get you to date him, to have sex with him. Why didn't you say anything to us?"

"Because I thought I could handle it. It was a mistake and I wish that I'd done things differently. I apologize for that."

"Water under the bridge. You need to thank your friend, Rebecca, who has been your strongest advocate while you've been gone. She and Preston have been singing your praises all over town."

Grace turned her gaze toward Rebecca, who was staring open-mouthed at Toffer. When she felt Grace's stare, she raised her eyebrows and smirked. Grace returned the smirk and turned a curious gaze on Preston. Becca blushed and turned away and Grace made a mental note to ask her friend about the man.

Medina smiled and shook Toffer's hand. "It's time to begin. We should be done with this pretty quickly."

The trustee quickly called the meeting to order. He read the reason for the meeting; the discussion of allegations of blackmail against Grace Kinison. The school's attorney, Carlton Bunch, read the charges and then explained to the parents who were present what steps were taken to investigate the accusations.

"We have taken several depositions from Ms. Kinison's students, both past and present, and found no one, save Mr. Markham and Mr. Barlow, who both later confessed that they had made the story up to get back at Ms. Kinison, whom they blamed for Mr. Barlow's failing grade last year. They said they waited until after Mr. Markham's class had turned in their term papers so that the charge would seem credible."

Preston nodded and some of the parents who were present grumbled.

"How do we know it's true?" One of the parents stood. "I mean this woman was just featured on the front of a tabloid having her breast fondled."

Toffer started to stand and Preston pushed him back into his chair. "Let me."

But before he could stand, a weak voice rang out.

"Can I say something?"

Grace turned her head toward the student who stepped forward, clasping her hands together to control the shaking.

"What is your name?" Medina asked.

"I'm Jessica LaBlonc. I'm one of Ms. Kinison's students. I'd like to say something good about her."

Grace bit her lip to keep from crying.

"Go ahead, Jessica," Medina said.

"I hate English. It's so hard, but I worked hard to get things done. In December, I was failing. Ms. Kinison helped me with my research paper. She stayed after school with me, working in the library to help me with research. She didn't do the work for me, but when I asked for help, she gave it. Thanks to her, I'm now passing. I don't care what nobody else says, she's a good teacher. The pictures don't matter. We just want her back."

Toffer grasped Grace's hand and smiled.

Discussion flew around the room and then Medina raised his hand. "Since this is an employment issue, the board is going to go into executive session to discuss things further. We will return with our decision on what to do about this matter in a short while. You're all welcome to stay if you want."

When the board left the room, Toffer was surrounded by people who wanted his autograph. Grace stepped aside and watched as he deftly handled the crowd. It was amazing to her that as Drake, he could come up with things to say at the drop of a hat. As Toffer, he'd stumbled and stuttered when Giselle had read from the paper.

"He's gorgeous," Becca said softly.

"And Preston?"

"We'll see."

The two giggled, and the both of them frowned as Watson stepped toward them. "I'm losing my job because of you."

"You're losing your job because you abused your power," Grace said. "I can't take the credit for that, although I would like to."

Watson opened his mouth to object, and then closed it when Toffer stepped forward. "I'd like to deck you, but I won't because of all the students present. It would set a very bad example. But if you ever say another foul thing to my wife again, or take a look at anything below her chin, I can't promise I'd be so reserved in my actions."

Watson stiffened, turned and walked back to his seat. Grace shook her head and laid her head on his shoulder.

"My hero."

Toffer nodded and kissed her cheek. "What are your plans for the rest of the school year?"

"I don't know." They hadn't discussed the issue and Grace gave him a questioning look.

"It's up to you, Grace. I will support you in whatever you decide."

She nodded and then bit her lip as the board came out of their private chambers. She had a huge decision to make, and she wasn't sure what she was going to do. But whatever happened she was glad that she had Toffer to stand by her side.

* * *

Grace turned up the heat in her apartment and then surveyed her surroundings.

"When the school year is out, I'll have a moving company pack things up to move to your house. Do you think that will work?"

Toffer sat in a large recliner and patted the arms of the chair. "I like this chair. If you decide to get rid of anything, make sure this isn't it."

Grace nodded. The board had come back and said they'd found Grace innocent of all charges. She'd been reinstated, and then Medina had smiled.

"We all know you've recently married, Ms. Kinison." The room erupted in applause and Grace smiled. "Despite the fact that your husband lives in California, we hope that you'll stay the rest of the school year with us."

Grace turned toward a group of her students, led by Jessica, and nodded. "I couldn't leave my team in midstream. I'll finish the year, with your permission."

Medina had smiled and the meeting had ended. Grace, Becca, Preston and Toffer had enjoyed a wonderful dinner at an expensive restaurant, and Grace grinned as she noticed the growing bond between Becca and Preston.

She and Toffer had agreed that she'd travel to California every other weekend. In the meantime, they'd have webcams installed at the house so they could keep in touch face to face, so to speak.

Now, back in her apartment, she shook her head. "Going to a school board meeting is hardly an exciting way to spend Valentine's Day."

"Well, perhaps this will help." Toffer pulled a long black box out of is pocket. "I seem to remember promising someone that after the party on Saturday we'd have an official collaring ceremony."

Grace nodded, biting her lip and then releasing it at Toffer's frown.

"We're going to have to break you of that habit of biting your lips. Take off all your clothes and kneel before me, Lolly."

Grace quickly stripped, kneeling before Toffer, who still sat in the chair, and spread her legs. He opened the box and Grace gasped.

Inside was a slim leather collar, inlaid with small diamond stones.

"Oh, Master, it's beautiful."

"Do you accept my collar, Grace?"

"Yes, Master."

He lifted it from its resting place and held it up in front of her face.

"Kiss it for me."

The leather was cool against her lips.

"Grace Kinison Shelley, I claim you as my submissive. You belong to me now, every delectable inch of your body, every inquiring part of your mind. I love you, Grace. I promise to guide you, train you, and provide for you in every way. You in turn will promise to obey me in every respect. Do you accept my collar, wife?"

"Yes, Master, I do."

Toffer clasped the leather around Grace's neck, and then kissed her gently.

"Well, we need to speak about that punishment that you have coming for running from me on Saturday."

"Shall I stand in the corner?"

"Oh no, Lolly. That's much too lenient. I'm thinking a meeting with the riding crop the next time you're at home."

Grace smiled. "Home."

"That's right, Grace. Home. Our home."

"Part of the punishment will be waiting so long. The anticipation until you get home will keep you on pins and needles. Don't you agree?"

"Whatever you say, Master. Whatever you say."

~ * ~

GRACEFUL MISCHIEF

Chapter One

Note to self: They say beauty is skin deep, but truly, beauty is more how you interact with other people. Truly beautiful people can be truly ugly when they open their mouths.

To do list: Finish edits on three chapters

Write M's story on favorite fantasies

Be ready for dinner at seven, sharp!

Grace Shelley stretched her arms above her head and arched her back. A day's worth of writing sometimes meant an aching back, but today she didn't have that problem. Since her first novel had been published two years ago, she'd been busy not only career-wise, but personally, too. She loved it. And today, she was excited about getting some alone time with her Master, her lover, her husband.

A warm glow filled her, despite the chill in the stone walls. She grinned as she toyed with the computer keys. She was in a castle, an honest-to-goodness English castle, with more rooms than she could count, wings that went off in all directions and hallways wide enough to fit a swimming pool.

She wouldn't be here if she wasn't married to one of the most handsome men in all of Hollywood, Toffer Shelley, known to the world as Drake Dawson, and known to Grace as Master, the man who kept her safe and provided her with innumerable pleasures. Most of all, though, he was the man who loved her exactly as she was.

For three and a half years now she'd been his wife, his lover, and his submissive. She'd obeyed his every command and was always hungry for more. It didn't matter to him that he was tall, dark and very, very handsome, and she herself was not so tall, nor so beautiful, and at size eighteen, not anywhere near as svelte as the wives of the other actors they knew. She had learned early in their marriage not to say anything derogatory about her size, because Master didn't like it, and she didn't like the punishments that came from those transgressions.

She'd also learned to ignore the tabloids and the reports on TV entertainment programs showing them on the red carpet, where the commentators made less than flattering remarks. Toffer dealt with it with perfect aplomb. If he heard the comments, or heard of them, he ignored that reporter the next time he saw them at an event, and would stick little comments in interviews about "small-minded people who had to feel better about themselves by cutting other people down."

The reporter would have to make some sort of apology before Toffer would give them the time of day again. Since he was one of Hollywood's leading men, they needed his stories to boost their ratings. Grace hugged herself, then looked at her watch. It was after five. She needed to bathe and then get dressed for dinner.

Toffer had told her he expected her to be ready at seven. Any later and he would construct a punishment fitting the crime. The idea made her smile, and she thought about leaving a button undone, or not having her shoes on when he arrived.

The idea was fun, but the idea of going to London for dinner held more interest for her. Since Toffer had started filming Days of Grace, a medieval love story, he'd worked fifteen-hour days. Tonight would be the first evening they'd had to go out together in weeks.

The fact it was Halloween only made things more exciting. This morning, Toffer had said something about going to a party in London, at a BDSM club. She'd smiled her approval, even as her heart had beat just a little bit too fast. They didn't generally go to public places, since there was too much of a chance of someone selling a photo of him inside the club to a tabloid.

But since it was Halloween, they could wear masks and not be recognized. She allowed her thoughts to wander about the pleasures that awaited, then realized with a start it was a quarter to six. She hurried to the bathroom and bathed, making sure everything was properly shaved, then tried to dress in a hurry, which wasn't easy to do considering she was hooking herself into a corset.

Toffer had bought her the bright red satin treat last weekend, saying he wanted her to wear it tonight. It was an over-the-bust style, so it could be worn in public. But once she looked at herself in the mirror, Grace shook her head. Her large breasts were almost overflowing the top and she knew she would be self-conscious, despite the fact she would be wearing a blouse over it.

She wanted to take it off, but Master would be disappointed. She closed her eyes and remembered his words after one program's criticism of her size. "What matters, Lolly-girl is that you're beautiful to me."

He'd gotten back at the reporter as only Toffer could do. He'd told his friends the man was insufferable, and he'd brought Grace to tears. At the next awards program, the confused journalist had been ignored by almost everyone he'd tried to corral for an interview, and had almost lost his job. Almost. Realizing what had happened, he'd apologized, then asked Toffer for an interview. He'd proceeded to do a glowing piece about how love had no boundaries, least of all the boundaries of size.

Grace put on her stockings, taking care to make sure she fastened each of them to the satin hooks hanging from the corset, then pulled on her skirt. She stepped into her high heels, something Toffer loved, and then last, but certainly not least, she changed the slim leather collar inlaid with diamonds she wore in private for a beautiful black collar with teardrop jewels hanging from it.

She wore a collar everywhere, and Toffer had made sure she had beautiful ones in different colors to match the outfits she wore. She was standing in front of the mirror, hoping her breasts didn't pop out sometime tonight, when the e-mail program on her computer dinged.

A check of her watch showed she had five minutes until Toffer arrived. He'd said he would shower and get ready in his trailer, and then come to pick her up. When his e-mail

address showed in her in-box she smiled. She opened the
mail and felt her heart lurch in her chest.

"You have five minutes to get to the entrance of the
maze. Don't worry about a purse, you won't need it. Just
make sure you're there, my Lolly-girl."

A giggle escaped her lips. Obviously, Toffer wanted to
play some before dinner, and that was just fine with her. She
checked her reflection in the mirror one more time and
headed out the door, hoping she remembered where to find
the maze and wasn't too late for Toffer's outing.

Chapter Two

It was almost ten minutes after seven when Grace found the entrance to the maze. Toffer was standing there, one leg bent backward, his foot resting on the thick hedge. He looked handsome as ever. His compelling face lit up with anticipation when Grace came into view, and her stomach did flip-flops. No matter how many times she saw him, it was always the same -- her palms would sweat and her heart would beat faster. It was hard to believe that the handsome man was her husband. Right now, he wore his dark hair just past his shoulders for the movie role. And he definitely wasn't dressed for dinner. He was wearing jeans and a pullover.

"Hello, my Grace." His voice was deep as she stopped in front of him. He cupped her cheek and kissed her lightly. "You're late."

"I'm sorry. I couldn't find…"

"No excuses." He stroked her arms, then pushed aside her shirt and traced his fingers over the edge of her breasts. Her nipples hardened in response.

"So beautiful, and all mine." His voice was deep. He gathered her close and caressed her hips, his breath hot against her neck. "Take off all your clothes, except for the corset and stockings, and of course, your shoes."

"Master, I…"

His upraised eyebrows stilled her words. She took off her shirt and dropped it on the bench, her skirt following. When she'd stepped out of her panties, he groaned in appreciation and she shivered. Her gaze darted from side to side to see if anyone was around.

"Don't worry. Everyone's up at the party." He reached inside of the corset and lifted each of her breasts out, setting them on top of the satiny material.

"I thought we were going to dinner, Master." His fingers caressed and kneaded her nipples, making her groan softly.

"Well, since it's Halloween I decided a little trick-or-treat was in order. I'm going to give you a three-minute head start, one for each glorious year you've been my wife. Then, I'm coming after you. If I catch you, I top you in the maze. If you make it to the center without being caught, then we go to dinner and play at the club."

He reached into his pocket and pulled out a silk tie. "Put your wrists together."

Grace did as she was told. The silk was cool on her wrists as he bound them closely together.

He pulled on the knot to make sure her wrists were secure.

He ran his finger down her belly and probed at the juncture of her thighs.

"Open for me."

She widened her stance and his finger dipped inside her pussy, wiggling through her wetness until he found her clit.

"Yes, you're very excited." He lifted his finger to her mouth and she sucked it inside, tasting her juices as he fucked her mouth slowly. When he pulled out and traced her lips, she groaned.

"Master, I…"

"Three minutes."

"…think we should…"

"Two fifty-nine, two fifty-eight, two fifty-seven."

Grace took a step back from him and then entered the maze. She could hear him counting as she turned the first corner, wishing she'd paid more attention to their host on the first day when he'd guided them to the middle. She knew there was a long stone table there, with chairs around it, but she had no idea how to find it.

The wind rustled the hedge and she stopped to take a deep breath. What would happen if someone else was already in the maze, playing a different game and they stumbled upon her, basically naked with her wrists tied in front of her?

She knew there were no children here at the house, so she didn't have to worry about that. But there was always the chance someone else was here. Maybe Cedric Davenport, Toffer's uber handsome co-star, who was also a Dom. Would her Master pull him into their game? In recent months they'd talked about him wanting to watch Grace with another man.

The idea excited Grace, too, but not like this. She wasn't prepared, mentally or physically. She stopped to get her bearings. She'd already made several wrong turns that led to dead-ends. It was fully dark outside, but low lamps lit several of the corners.

She'd just eyed a trail that looked vaguely familiar when Toffer's voice reached her ears.

"Ready or not, here I come."

Had it already been three minutes? Grace tried to slow her breathing as she headed for the path. She wanted to go to London for dinner, and to visit the club. To do that, she had to beat Toffer to the middle. And she wasn't going to do it just standing here.

Chapter Three

The damp earth below her swallowed her heels as she rounded the next corner. She almost lost her balance, placing her bound hands against the shrubbery to steady herself. She glanced to the left and was heartened to see several lights she was sure marked the center of the maze.

A few steps and she would be there, she was sure of it. She'd found the center, which amazed her. Toffer's game had been fun, but it would be treat time instead of trick. She smiled to herself and pulled up her leg, her foot coming out of her shoe, which stayed stuck in the muck.

She bent over to pull the heel out. She'd just stepped into it again when Toffer's low whistle wrapped itself around her.

"Now there's a beautiful sight. If I didn't already have games planned, I'd fuck you right here."

"Master."

"That's right, Grace, it's your Master. And he's come to claim his prize." He ran his hand over her bare behind.

"How did you find me so fast?"

"Because I'm good, Gracie, and because I'm motivated by the thought of fucking you here, where anybody could come up and see us." He stepped in front and pulled a long, black silk scarf from his pocket. He wound it through her bindings and started to walk toward the center, leading her by her bound wrists.

He took several turns, without missing a beat, before stopping at the entrance to the center. Grace stared at the table. It had indeed been prepared for her, with bindings on the bottom legs, and a cord that ran the length of it.

"Put your ass right on the edge of the table, my love. Then lie back with your legs spread over either edge and raise your arms above your head."

Grace didn't argue. Gone was the idea of going to London. She was thrilled with the "trick" her Master was playing on her. She stayed silent as he bound her spread legs to either table leg, and then replaced the black silk scarf with the rope and secured her arms above her head. Her pussy was right on the edge, in a perfect spot for her Master to enter. Her breasts were held in place by the corset. She was firmly on display.

"Remain silent and still, unless I speak to you, do you understand me, Lolly?"

"Yes, Master."

Her body tingled at his voice, deep and commanding. "No matter what happens, or what is said. I know you can do it, my sweet one."

"Thank you, Master."

He leaned over and kissed her, his lips soft against her own. Then he placed the black scarf over her eyes and things went black.

Grace sucked in her breath and bit her lip to keep from crying out. Being blindfolded in their home was one thing, but being blindfolded in the middle of a maze in the English countryside was another. It set her nerves on end. She loved her Master, and she knew he loved her. She also trusted him with her body and soul. She knew he would never do anything to hurt her, but right now she was totally outside her comfort zone.

It was both terribly frightening and thrilling at the same time. She knew he was watching her, waiting for her to become accustomed to her position. Her clit throbbed in anticipation and her nipples grew even tighter.

After what seemed an eternity, but was probably only a few minutes, he traced his fingers over her stomach and down her leg. She felt his presence at the end of the table, her senses heightened by the blindfold.

Toffer tickled the insides of her thighs before moving up to run his finger along her wet slit. He slipped inside and caressed her soft flesh, stopping just short of her clit.

"Yummy," he said softly. When the tip of his tongue flickered across her engorged bud she almost cried out. Almost. Over the last three years she'd learned to be good and to follow her Master's directions.

He replaced his tongue with his thumb, pushing her clit into her flesh, moving the hard nub around before taking the pressure away totally. Grace's body was on fire, her need to come threatening to overtake her discipline in obeying her Master.

When his tongue flicked out again she sighed.

"Bad Lolly," he said, a chuckle in his voice. "Tell me, did you write my stories about your fantasies?"

A rustling in the trees made Grace tense.

"Not yet, Master."

"I know your real work interfered, but I want my stories soon."

The rustling noise intensified. *Was someone there?*

"Of course, you know my fantasy, don't you?"

"Yes, Master. To watch me with another man."

"That's right, Gracie. Explain to me again why the idea makes you so uncomfortable."

Her entire body was tense. There was someone else there. She heard footsteps padding against the soft earth, coming closer to them.

Fears about her size and another person's reaction surfaced. She knew Toffer loved her, and loved her body. She was comfortable with her size around him, but not around others. Now she knew someone was watching, looking at her as she was tied to a table, her legs spread, her nipples hard.

Toffer slapped her pussy. "Answer me, Grace."

"Master, I'm too big for things like that."

Toffer slapped her pussy again, and again. Grace moaned. "And I think you're absolutely beautiful, just the way you are. What do you think, my friend? Am I right, or is she?"

Grace pulled on her bindings as Cedric Davenport's voice rang out.

"She's extraordinary. She looks good enough to eat."

"Doesn't she? She's so very tasty. We've had this discussion for a while now about playing with others. I've deferred to Grace's insecurities about her size, but no more. It's time for my wife to learn she's beautiful in so many ways. I hated to trick her into it, but I knew even tonight, at the club, she would have balked at being naked."

Grace's stomach roiled. He'd never intended to take her to the club, never intended them to have a night in London. This had been his plan all along. She felt a little betrayed, but at the same time, she knew he'd done this because he knew her so well. He'd been right. Even at the club she would have not wanted to be naked, and that would have led to a fight, and a punishment.

Cedric began to slide the silk scarf from her face, tugging it gently at the end so it fell. When it was gone his smiling face came into view. He was truly handsome. An actor known for his action movies who, at the age of forty-two, still had the buff body of a twenty-year-old. Not only was he known for his movies, but for the fact he dated twenty-something starlets who looked like they'd never put more than a grape in their mouth for a meal.

"Hello, Grace."

"Cedric." Her hands were sweating.

Toffer's hands were on her thighs, gently stroking them up and down, tickling her with his fingertips. Grace looked down at him. He winked at her, and then lowered his head down, his tongue assaulting her clit with new abandon.

Grace tried to lie still, tried not to look at Cedric, who had turned his gaze toward Toffer's head as her husband licked her clit, and then inserted two fingers into her wetness, fucking her with them as his tongue danced around her.

"Come for me, Grace." His voice was muffled. "Come for us. Move around. Be loud. Be my beautiful Lolly."

Toffer's words sent chills up her spine as he continued to lap at her clit. She closed her eyes and concentrated on the sensations. She thought back to when she and Toffer were first together. After their marriage, he still had to coax her into being naked, going so far as to tell her she had to spend entire weekends naked for his pleasure.

He'd complimented her, told her how graceful she was, how tantalizing and delicious. Was she graceful now? Did that change just because Cedric was watching her? She shook her head, knowing that it didn't. She was still beautiful. She still hadn't learned what her Master was trying to teach her. No matter what others thought of her, she was beautiful to him, and that made her gorgeous.

She bucked against his tongue, licking her own lips as if to join his.

"Oh, Master. So good." Toffer's tongue circled her nub, then he sucked it into his mouth, biting it gently, taking it between his teeth and rubbing the edge of his tongue back and forth.

"Master! May I come?"

Toffer nodded, his tongue still working her quivering flesh. Grace flew over the edge, her body quaking in delight at the idea her Master loved her, and someone was watching.

"Master! Master! Oh, Master!" She bucked and pulled against her bonds as wave after wave of bliss washed over her, leaving her weak and content. He pushed harder and Grace came a second time.

"Toffer!"

She continued to yell his name, not caring who heard, or what they would think. She didn't care that she would receive punishments for using his real name, and not calling him Master. She wanted him to know how much she loved him, and how much pleasure he was bringing her.

"Damn." Cedric said in awe. "How do you make a woman come like that, Toffer?"

Toffer licked her clit again, then lifted his head. "By loving her."

Chapter Four

Grace sat on the edge of the table, her Master nestled between her thighs. He rubbed each of her wrists, then kissed them gently.

"Are you feeling all right?"

"Yes, Master."

"Physically and mentally?"

She gave him a beaming smile. "Yes."

"Good. I'd hoped you wouldn't be too angry with me."

She shook her head. "No, Sir."

"Promise? Because if I find out you're just saying that, you know what happens, right?"

Grace nodded. She knew if she lied about her feelings, Toffer always found out. Above all, he wanted honesty between them where feelings were concerned.

"You know my fantasy, don't you?"

"Yes, Master."

He kissed the tip of her nose, then stepped back. "Ced, I hope you brought a condom."

"Several," Cedric said with a laugh. "Strawberry, or cherry flavored?"

Grace buried her face in her hands, her shoulders shaking with laughter.

"Strawberry," Toffer said, his gaze focused on Grace. "She loves them."

Grace shivered when Cedric's fingers traced her shoulder blades. Toffer stepped away and she wanted to reach out for him, to draw him closer.

"It's been my fantasy for some time, Cedric, to watch Grace with another man. To watch her get pleasure from him, knowing he found her attractive."

Cedric kissed her shoulder. "She's stunning. And the way she gives of herself, with such abandon." He turned Grace gently, but she kept her gaze on Toffer. When Cedric captured a nipple in his mouth and sucked it in she gasped. Toffer hissed and nodded, his hand going down to stroke his cock.

He undid his pants as Cedric moved to her other nipple. He went back and forth between them as Toffer took his cock out and began to stroke it, his gaze fastened on his wife's breasts.

"Oh, Master."

Toffer laughed. "Me? What about Cedric? Let him know you're enjoying his attentions."

Grace turned her face to the good-looking star. He lifted his gaze to her and smiled before dropping back to recapture a nipple. He bit it gently and she shivered, running her hands through his hair and then over his naked back.

Her eyes widened when she realized he was naked. When had that happened? She guessed when she was talking with Toffer. She shifted her head so she could see his cock. It stood proud and erect, covered in red latex.

"I want to touch you. Feel you."

Cedric took a step back and nodded. Grace looked to Toffer for approval before dropping to her knees in front of the man. She stroked his cock, savoring the sighs that came from both men. She wiggled her tongue against the tip of his erection, then opened her lips and sucked him inside.

"Yes, Grace, suck him."

She put her hands on his hips, taking him in as far as she could before pulling back and sucking him back inside.

His hands were gentle on her hair and Toffer's loud "fuck, yes," sent rockets of satisfaction through her body.

"He wanted you, Grace. We were discussing fantasies, just as you and I have been doing, and when I said I wanted to watch my wife with another man, he volunteered. He said he thought you were scrumptious."

"I was right," Cedric said.

Grace moaned around his cock. The strawberry flavor from the condom was delicious, and when she felt Toffer's hands on her shoulders pulling her back and lifting her to her feet she groaned in disapproval.

"You'll have him back soon enough, my wife. Besides, we have all night."

Cedric climbed onto the table, taking the exact position Grace had, except he had no restraints.

"Suck him again." She bent over and took him in her mouth. He seemed larger this time, his hand on her head as he stroked her hair the same way her lips stroked his cock, back and forth, back and forth.

Toffer's hands grasped her hips as he positioned her for his entry. He slid inside her in one hard stroke, making Grace squeal with delight around the throbbing cock in her mouth. The rhythm was hard and steady, Cedric sliding into her mouth at the same time Toffer slid out of her pussy, then the reverse happening.

"Play with your clit." Toffer's voice was heavy with desire.

Grace's fingers dropped to her aching clit. It pulsated against her fingers as she stroked it, wet with her own juices and with the remnants of Toffer's saliva.

"I'm going to come," Cedric said. Grace panicked for a moment, until she remembered the condom. Then she tightened her lips, sucking him in deeper as Toffer slammed himself into her harder and harder.

"Fuck!" Cedric's cock seemed to expand in her mouth as he shot off. The strawberry flavor was all Grace tasted, and seconds later Toffer muttered the same word, the sounds of their flesh slamming into each other filling the small enclosed space.

When Toffer had stopped thrusting, and Cedric had collapsed onto the table, Toffer's fingers linked with Grace's to rub her nub.

"Did you like that, my love?"

"I did."

"Me, too." Cedric's voice made them all laugh. He sat up and captured Grace's nipples between his thumbs and forefingers.

"Come, my Grace. Show me your enjoyed your little trick."

She could feel it building inside her, the pressure from hands on her breasts and fingers on her clit too much to bear.

"Master!" She came in a rush of power as both men increased their stimulation of her body. When the orgasm stopped pounding through her, she realized her head rested on Cedric's thigh and both men were stroking her back.

"Shall we retire inside," Toffer said. "I think we have a few more treats to explore tonight."

Grace moaned softly. With Toffer, each experience was more memorable than the last. Even when he was being tricky, she seemed to get all the treats. She shivered under their caresses and knew that this would be a Halloween to remember.

 **THE END**

Melinda Barron

Melinda Barron loves to explore Egyptian tombs and temples, discover Mayan ruins, play in castles towers, and explore new cities and countries. She generally does it all from the comfort of her home by opening a book.

Melinda is the fourth of five children born to an Army officer and his wife. A longtime newspaper journalist, Melinda has loved to read and write from an early age. Now she lives in the Texas Panhandle with two cats, Amelia and Pippin, and enough books to, according to her brother, open her own library. In addition to reading and writing Melinda enjoys travel, cross-stitching, watching movies and spending time with her friends and family.

LaVergne, TN USA
05 May 2010
181616LV00002B/68/P